"*Malcriada & Other Stories* is an uppercut to the [...]
debut collection."
--Elizabeth Acevedo, author of *The Poet)*

"In *Malcriada*, Lorraine Avila, offers every ounce [...] attitude, and deep
reckoning a woman can offer in the face of a world that's constantly trying to
stomp her out. Malcriada is the snap of her jaws claiming the life she mother-
f*cking deserves. Avila's writing is coming for us all."
-- Gabby Rivera, author of *Juliet Takes a Breath*

"Avila's writing is a soul-stirring experience, as she navigates trauma with
deep care, while exalting women and treating us like poetry, allowing us to
breathe even as we dive deep into the lives of her characters."
--Amanda Alcántara, author of *Chula*

"*Malcriada & Other stories*" is a courageous and bold compilation of
stories breaking barriers within the Dominican diaspora. Any Dominican
migrant will find themselves in Avila's words and call it home. I wept, ached,
and healed with her characters. Every story brought me closer to the parts
of me the diaspora had swallowed hole. I remembered the innocence and
harshness of living in the island, along with the joy and loss of leaving. Avila
sparks many important conversations about the layers of abuse, the
challenge of recovery, and the triumph of growth. Every young Dominican
woman needs a copy of this book to annotate and turn to when a ticket to
the homeland is not an option. In these stories, I found all the women I have
been and hope to become. --Danyeli Del Orbe, Poet

In "*Malcriada*," Lorraine Avila guides you into a journey that you never want to
end.

In her first story, titled after her book, Lorraine tackles the complexity and
depth of illegal immigration; she touches on the nuances of feminism in
"Bodysuit;" and shares a love story intertwined with anti-blackness and self-
care in "Justice."

You'll meet a variety of women—and a few men—every one of them
different than the last. Yet even in their very obvious differences, you'll find
something about each of them that gives you a feeling of déjà vu — almost as
if you've met them before. Even in their worst moments, you'll love them all.

The voices used in *Malcriada* will remind you of your own. The memories
shared will cause you to dig up those that you've unknowingly buried.
Avila's ability to capture the experience of a recent immigrant, the intricacy
of a relationship between two best friends, and the pain of anyone who's
been hurt by someone they loved, is remarkable.
--MP Frias, author of *The Art of Letting Go*

MALCRIADA & OTHER SHORT STORIES
Copyright © 2019 Lorraine Avila
ISBN-13: 978-0-578-49119-6

Cover Art and Internal Art: Crystal Rodriguez
Editor: Sydney Valerio
Book Designer: Eneas Núñez
Headshot Photographer: Amanda Sade

DWA Press: www.dwapress.com
An Imprint of the Dominican Writers Association
www.dominicanwriters.com
Email: info@dominicanwriters.com

MALCRIADA

& other stories

by Lorraine Avila

Para Mamá Gladys quien sabía que yo era una escritora antes que cualquier otra cosa, y quien vio una niña poderosa cuando otros me llamaban Malcriada.

And for all Malcriadxs worldwide.

*"I know how to reach difficult places,
how to be broken and put together again."*
- Aja Monet, "What I've Learned"

In the seventh grade, I was kicked out of middle school. Kicked out for fighting, or inciting, or whatever the assistant principal put together on the statement that Mami could not understand but still blamed me entirely for-it affirmed the idea that I was really a Malcriada. Tan malcriada that even the gringos and their Departments of Education did not know what to do with me.

In middle school, I was the kid playing tug of war between English and Spanish, trying to wedge into somewhere, with Muslim best friends who stole henna from their moms for me on one side and the neighborhood turn up queens trying to be initiate me on the other. On some days, you could find me, all during lunch, at tables passing my spiral notebook around with stories that were trying to yell something. Or on the yard sitting with my back lying against the gate reading a book. Or cursing someone out or pulling hair. Or missing my dad. Or making out with boys. Or thinking of girls. Or rolling my eyes. Or crying. Or having friends break up with me because I was always changing. Or making my mother and stepfather cry. Or fighting my sister. Or harming myself. Or telling my grandmother where it hurt. Or listening to my grandfather play his guitar in the living room until it annoyed me. Or introducing the vinegar and cebolla dressing to my Black American best friend. Or exploring myself. Or playing 50 cents' *Get Rich or Die Trying*. Or jamming to Aventura's *Love and Hate*. Or being angry. Or on the 4 train traveling through boroughs just to go to school. Or climbing on the pyramid on my way home. Or trying to grow up. Or remembering something that I had put away in order to exist.

Through the years, I have journeyed through a multitude of phases. In each of them, I have been trying to make up for something—and just recently I realized I've been trying to prove I am not that girl. But I am. I've always been Malcriada.

This collection is an ode to me. To all the Malcriadas in me that knew storytelling was where it was at for us to mitigate the heavy. I say all of this to say that while you read these stories, know that they were written for me before they were revised and given to you.

—

Malcriada. Ni de aquí, ni de allá. I was born and raised in the Bronx. A daughter of Dominicans. A chunk of my years growing up were always spent in el Cibao, so I grew up always feeling like there was no place I could be fully wedged into; a gringa there, a Dominican here and a Morenota everywhere. But one common thread—on the island and in the borough that saw me through was the label Malcriada. It managed to infiltrate the minds and exit mouths of folks here and there when they heard of me or interacted with me. It managed to cross oceans, generations, and differing opinions and became a second skin.

At first, it made me feel like an outcast. Next, it set my sister and I aside. Later, it insulted the people who came together to raise me. Most of the times, it was the village that raised me that labeled me this, pero así es la vida. It was a twisting of internal hate I couldn't comprehend. But that weight of being Malcriada lived heavy in my underbelly, in my chest. Even when I managed to do what was asked of me, to exceed the steps of my predecessors, having an opinion and voicing it, made me a Malcriada.

Being a girl with wants, needs, and desires made me crooked. *This notion still finds ways to live in me now. I am still shedding.* I just don't apologize for it anymore.

Malcriada.

Poorly raised.

Raised badly.

It's a hell of a thing to call kids who don't have the multitude of resources needed to navigate the world in the shape that it's handed over to those born in these bodies.

This coming of age narrative isn't mine alone. This label has followed too many of us. It has altered our understanding of others and others' understanding of us. The damage, for me, lies in what it does to us individually—it forces us to see the worst in ourselves before seeing the great in our cores.

The blessing in this mix up is that we, as a generation have been pushed to this—we are powerful things that cannot be tamed by tradition or white-washed innovation. The external world, along with our understanding of it from these bodies, may taint and ache, but only we know what it takes to liberate ourselves.

This collection of short stories is an intimate entryway into a series of characters that have been poorly raised, handed the shorter end of the stick, but still managed to hang onto something— sisterhood, art, love, faith, social mobility, pleasure, self-healing—to make it through.

Bare with me, the wounds must be examined to get the cure.

Pa' lante—

Lorraine Avila

((

●

Malcriada

The sun was lazy and still deciding on whether or not to illuminate the Caribbean when Malcriada found herself on a wooden boat with eighteen other passengers and two captains. There was a line of promises to a thriving future, if and only if they could surpass the upcoming turmoil that would anchor them to this boat. As Malcriada's back rubbed up against the splinters of the wooden structure, her skin threatened to split wide open.

It was between the painful sunburn and the constant timid flowing of the ocean that Malcriada decided to bite her tongue for the first time. Instead, she stuffed her ears with her fingertips. She didn't want to listen to the screams and the ripping of skin. Muffled cries and shouts came from the left of her, and she dared to just slightly open her eyes. The open sea was still the open sea—vastly threatening and soft. The beast arrived a glossy planet made of silt clay. Malcriada watched the school of fish, who had made the bottom of the boat a university, disappear as if they were escaping dry land itself. She unplugged her fingertips from her ears. The bleeding woman frantically reached up trying to take hold of the boat as the thought of the sea creature had come just for her ruled her every move. In an unintentional motion, she struck it with her knee as it attempted to chase after the injured fish.

Miguel and the other captain had decided to throw the pregnant girl overboard when she first started to bleed. Through a single locking of eyes, they had agreed that it was too late; the fish had gathered underneath them, rubbed up against the wood, and expelled enough of their own blood to attract the sharks, who usually minded their business. The sharks had arrived slowly. They had come merely for the fish, but Miguel knew enough to know that eventually they would become curious of the humans. The bleeding girl, who was 19 and traveled with her twin sister, was the only way to save the rest.

The tiger shark went in for the win of her swollen womb. 48 teeth made their way deep into her skin. As soon as it got the taste of human blood, it released her. The second beast, overestimating the danger its kin was under, took a chunk of her arm. Although Malcriada tried to turn away at this point, she saw the pink tone of bone from the shallow heights of the yola. Every single body on the yola moaned in pain as if it was them who the sea creatures had gotten the chance to taste. Miguel and the captain had to hold down the twin sister who convulsed while giving birth to grief.

☾

Malcriada was born with a large mouth. The edges of her lips stretched to the mid area of her cheeks and when she smiled you'd think her lips could kiss her ears. A banana could fit from edge to edge when her white teeth came together to crack a smile. She had tested this. Her lips were plump, the color of plum and she sometimes sucked on them swearing to be tasting a fruit she had never actually tasted. She imagined plum tasted like sweet blood and mud. And when she spoke the truth, which was often, her tongue cultivated the foreign taste over and over again.

Malcriada didn't know her name. Because ever since she had uttered her first word, ¡Mamá!, no one could stand the tone in her voice. No one could accept a child with a mouth of such considerable size and a brain so apparently small could scream and demand something she felt the need to have. The day she said her first word was when her mother made the decision to go to the coast of the island and board the yola towards Puerto Rico.

Malcriada's mother placed her on the middle of the table and stretched out her own dress before she sat across from her vecina to tell her the news. She threw her head back in laughter filled with exhilarating disbelief.

Imagínate—yo una muchacha de el Cibao díque en Nueva Yoi. She shuffled her bare feet towards the stove and turned off the fire that boiled el agua para el café. La vecina tried to play peek-a-boo with Malcriada, but Malcriada looked at her—already bored of games. After having served the coffee, Malcriada's mother sat back down. The coffee cups the women brought to their lips were delicate and small, a staple that had been passed down from a part of the family lineage who was not in a rush to escape the Caribbean. Malcriada's mother carried on with the conversation.

Malcriada began to struggle with phonetic errors trying to enunciate the word her grandmother had been repeating for weeks. The sounds disrupted the conversations, and her mother sucked her teeth. Still, Malcriada continued making sound after sound, struggling to say the word her mother mouthed so many times as well when she was in a better mood. The sounds continued until the word that would shape the first twelve years of her life conquered her tiny tongue, ¡MAMÁ! ¡MAMÁ! ¡MAMÁ!

Esta niña no me deja ni pensar. ¿Me vas a gastar el nombre? Coñoooo, her mother scolded. Malcriada yelled for her mother again accentuating the final vowel as if it was that sound what would get her mother's attention.

¡Mira, Malcriada, cállate! Her mother turned to her, with a hand spread wide threatening the air, as her small toddler said her first word for a fourth time in a row. And that was that.

Malcriada stuck even on the days Malcriada
tried her very best not to talk.

☾

    Girls, good girls, talked in whispers. And in
the best-case scenario didn't say a word. They sat.
Their legs pressed against each other even when
the inside of their thighs peeled. They folded their
hands on their lap even when they wanted to reach
for something. They walked into a room and said
hello to every adult, even the ones who looked at
them in a way that made their stomachs turn.
Good girls besaban la mano and understood they
had to ask for blessings even from the ones who
had never been the recipients of any themselves.
Good girls looked down at the floor because that's
where they belonged.

    Malcriada wasn't a good girl. She tried to
keep the things she knew inside, but they piled up
until she yelled. Pateaba el piso como que el fuego
se formaba bajo de sus pies. She didn't like not
saying what she felt because she felt everything.
She felt everything a lot. Her mother had left for
Nueva York when she wasn't even two, and
something within Malcriada knew she would take
forever to send for her. In the meantime, her
grandmother, hit her with the branches of Jasmine
that grew in their garden when she could not help
the truth from rising up her throat.

    At first, the whips to her legs felt like a
million splinters, but by the time she reached the

end of elementary school, the lashes felt like a feather from a rooster. A soothing.

Her grandmother se montaba. And that is when Malcriada transformed herself to a good girl for as many seconds at a time as she could afford. She would conciliate her grandmother, get her to the bed, call for help in a tone that didn't scare people too much.

In the morning, Malcriada's grandmother would say something that felt like love, like ¿Qué haría yo sin ti? or Gracias hija. But by noon, it was back to normal because Malcriada asked too much. She asked what was for lunch? She asked who was Papa Candelo? She asked if she could go to the park with her amigas after el colegio? She asked why her parents never cared? When all these questions filled her chest.

Malcriada didn't feel, hear, or see her fate. Bonao, she was sure, was where she would stay. Even though Mami had fled, Mami never really wanted her, so why would Mami ever send for her anyway?

She was twelve when her mother called from a Banca central in Nueva York. Her abuela told her mother that it was time to send for her.

If Malcriada is going to make anything of herself, she should complete el bachillerato with the gringos over there not here. Malcriada heard her grandmother's voice and imagined herself aboard a bird who floated in the air and was pushed by the wind into a place far from the island that had formed her.

She found out quickly she wouldn't take the strange bird for the first wing of the trip. Instead she would take the same route her mother had taken ten years before. La yola. Malcriada's mother had loved a man on her journey towards Borinquen. She told Malcriada he was trustworthy. He had charged her the same he charged everyone, $450 American dollars, despite their history, but the most important thing was that he wasn't a fresco. When she reached Puerto Rico a family friend would pick her up near the beach they would land in. They had a Boricua identification card with a picture of a girl that looked just like Malcriada did in the picture from el colegio she sent her mother two years ago.

On the day she left, the callejón was quiet. The sun still slept behind las lomas and the roosters did not feel the need to wake anyone just yet. A blue camioneta came to the front of their house. Malcriada took in the smell of her grandmother's aged curtains and felt the cracking cement on the soles of her feet for what she knew would be the last time. At the door, she put on the sneakers her grandmother had haggled a cousin for. Her mother had sent an extra 150 dollars Americanos and her grandmother told her to stuff them into her bra. La vieja also gave her a school bookbag with three pairs of new underwear, a pair of pants, an extra dress, three shirts, and a thin windbreaker. Her grandmother told her the jacket would come in handy on the yola. At the top of the backpack were three containers: one filled with avena, another with plátano hervido con longaniza, and the last held two pans de agua with mayonnaise and fried salami. Malcriada had never seen so much food at once.

At the door, la vieja tapped her forehead, the space between her chest, and her shoulders, Que dios te acompañe, mi niña. Malcriada took a deep breath noticing her grandmother had not called her Malcriada but hers. When they exhaled, the knot in their throats softened as the tears flowed. La vieja held her to her chest, and Malcriada thought she was in heaven, resting on a cloud.

Yo siempre te he querido, mi niña, la vieja said. Que no se te borre este callejón de tu memoria. Que no se te olvide que fui yo y este callejón que te dio tu tamaño. Don't forget that if you make it out there, in that city bigger than our country, it is your duty to help la gente like us. La vieja tapped on her vascular and dark forearm. Malcriada hugged her grandmother and opened her mouth wanting to scream because the ache filled her chest, but nothing would come. She couldn't name the tearing of her stomach and the new feeling of responsibility.

☾

She had only seen the ocean two other times. When the eighteen other people mounted the small boat, she envisioned the ocean having them by lunch. But she proceeded knowing there was no use in trying to go back. Miguel was the man in charge. He wore rolled up jeans and a striped tank top. His mustache was dark and his black hair ended at his shoulder blades. He had a smile that immediately made her feel like not all men were the same. Once they were two miles in, he settled inside the edge of the wooden boat with her.

We have 273 miles to go, he said, if you're wondering. He took out a wall calendar he had rolled in the back pocket of his jeans. Hoy es 22 de junio de 1980, we'll get there early morning on this day, he pointed to the 27th.

Five days? That's a whole lot of time for all these people to be together on the same boat without using the bathroom, she blurted out louder than she expected to. Everyone turned to Miguel then because no one had bothered to ask that question pushed into the excitement of escape.

Bueno, Malcriada, he said standing up, what we do is cagar in these bags and pee into these containers and everything goes into the ocean.

☾

Later that night, as the yola danced slowly under the stars, the ocean resembled what Malcriada imagined being the edge of the world.

How many times you've done did this? She crouched next to Miguel and asked. Running his fingers through his wavy curls, Miguel thought of how high he should go to make this girl feel safe. But he didn't want to lie. She looked at him as she waited for an answer—her eyes urged him to be honest, as if she had insight that was too vigilant to believe anything that strayed from the truth.

58, he answered. Miguel took a deep breath.

In how much time? she asked. Malcriada's thick eyebrows rose and her eyes widened with more questions.

Since I was 15, so 18 years or so, más o menos. Instantly he remembered that he had first been sent to Puerto Rico on Caribair to study chemistry at la Universidad de Puerto Rico on a scholarship. Scholarships were nearly non-existent, and he was only in high school; his vieja had been so proud. Como cambian las cosas, he thought to himself.

Someone ever die? Malcriada's hands were cupped together on her lap. She had tried her best to swallow the question, but it had floated out of her before she had a chance to hold it back.

That's a hard question for a chamaquita to ask, in the middle of the ocean, to a man in the dark, Miguel chuckled.

My name is Malcriada. I'm not really scared of anything. She leaned back, stretching her back against the frame of the boat.

Not even the ocean? Miguel winked. She looked out into the sea. Her grandmother told her the stories of a woman who wears yellow, lots of gold, and guards the sweet waters with las ciguapas. She wondered if she was out here protecting the salty waters, and if she wasn't, then as she sat on the creaking boat, she would protect it for her.

The ocean is a friend. Look at how long it has held up our island. And how it is giving us permission to go from one island to the next. Permission the gringos won't even give us over our own waters. Malcriada took a deep breath tired of having to break down intelligible knowledge to adults who seldom wanted to understand.

Miguel looked at his palms, filled with blisters. He had made it a science to cross the waters, and here was a girl of twelve with soft hands making it a religion.

Too many people have died, he rubbed his palms together, I don't think they would consider these waters friendly. The passengers who had crossed to the other world in the middle of their crossing to Puerto Rico came to mind; island hopping, hoping to find an entryway into a country that did not want them. He laughed out loud uncomfortably.

Some of our ancestors, Malcriada said, the ones who never had a choice about entering the water, even they would argue it is men who ruin the sea and the soil for all of us. Miguel shook his head with a slight hint of disbelief.

Don't tell me ¿Eres media brujita? That must be why your mother thought you'd be able to handle this on your own.

☾

Malcriada napped for four hours, and she woke only when the waves turned her stomach. By morning, it asked for something. The pan de agua with salami her grandmother had wrapped up in papel de aluminio was what she reached for, but with the tips of her fingers she felt another kind of paper. As she pulled it out, she noticed it was a single lined paper ripped out from one of her notebooks. She unfolded it slowly and gently as if she were opening something fragile.

Her grandmother's crooked script alarmed her. What could be so important she had to struggle to write? La vieja had only learned how to write a few years ago when Malcriada learned in school and taught her.

Mi'ja,

Si algún día encuentras la fuerza para perdonarme, te pido que lo hagas. La verdad es que yo te e tratado mal. Mal porque tengo miedo. Miedo porque yo era como tú, llena de ideas y verdad, y por mi sabiduría lo perdí todo. Tú no eres Malcriada. Lo que pasa es que tu sabes demasiado. El mundo no es justo, pero es sumamente malo para las niñas que nacen con poder y mucha curiosidad. Tu nombre no es Malcriada. Tu nombre es Naomi. Te nombre yo porque tu madre no sabía que inventarse entre el dolor y la sangre. Toma el nombre, y cuando te digan Malcriada, sigue directo porque lo que dicen no es para ti.

Con amor tu abuela,
La Malcriada Mayor

Out in the middle of the Caribbean Sea, Malcriada did not know if it was her tears, her sweat, or the water that splashed on her face that she felt rolling down her cheeks and dressing her lips in salt. She sucked on her bottom lip to soothe herself. She tasted sweet blood and mud. She wondered if Nueva York had the plums she had once seen on the posters plastered en el colegio. They were purpura and round.

¿Todo bien, Malcriada? Miguel asked her. She examined the sky as if it were preparing to come down on them. Despite her burning pupils, she kept her face pointed up towards all that existed above her. The sun gave her wet kisses and finally forced her to close her eyes.

If she wasn't Malcriada, if she was no longer a girl that had grown behaviorally malformed, that had been raised badly, then she could do and be anything. She opened her arms and took in the heat and the possibility.

Miguel, mi nombre es Naomi.

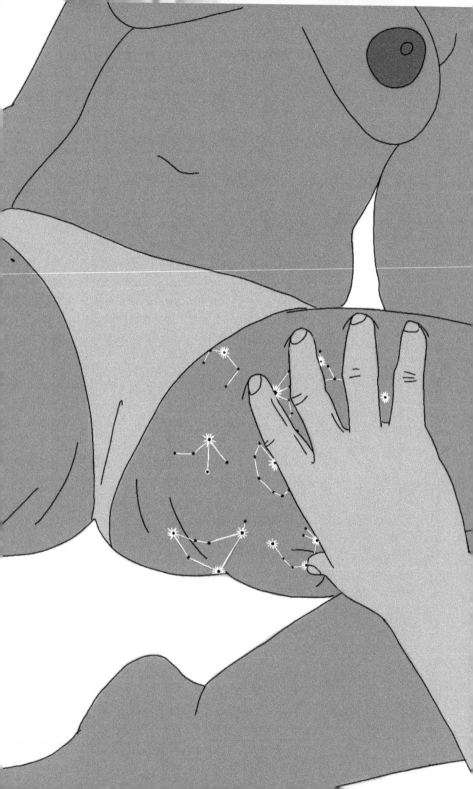

Nereyda's Stars

The first time Nicanor saw the stars on Nereyda's thighs he could not believe that God had decided to stamp a constellation on a woman. He just could not comprehend why God had gone out of his way to confuse him and his relationship to nature. That the thing that tamed his heart existed not only in the soil beneath his feet, the cacao that once rolled off his hands, and the heavens above his head but now also lived in a woman. Confused he breathed in deep taking all of her scents with him. He had failed to notice Nereyda, and now she was spread in front of his face like a poem. He moved forward kissing the stars on the darkness of her inner thigh.

After, he couldn't decide between laying with the woman or lying to her about having to go. So instead he closed his eyes. And let a woman, for the first time, decide.

☾

Nereyda had watched Nicanor's pattern with women for months. After all, he was not a stranger, he was her neighbor. She lived in the basement of a three-story house in Astoria. And he lived right above her with his sister and his brother in law. When they invited her to the parties they threw upstairs, she would go—claro que yes. He always danced with her. No one could sweep the floor in Salsa as she could. He joked with her. No one had a better smile or a better sense of humor than her. And after everyone had gone, he knew he could count on her to help him clean up. It was to her, and only her, he would reveal how much he missed working the land back home. For a while, all he wanted to do was enter La Gran Manzana and work like the men on la televisión. Now, he spent all of his days organizing plastic and styrofoam inside of a factory that operated like a prison. She listened, but it always ended there. For her.

He would then send a pager, and in less than half an hour a woman would knock on his door. It was always a different one. When the woman arrived, Nereyda heard their footsteps make their way to his room. Downstairs, if she stood near the boiler long enough, she could hear them moan.

☾

Today, she had found him at the bodega. Stroking the bodega cat with gleaming eyes. She took him by the hand, led him to the house, and opened her front door for him.

And now here he was lying next to her, their sweaty limbs hardly touching, and she was certain he was empty of love.

Even though she enjoyed the way he excavated for God in her, she didn't want an empty version of who she imagined him to be. He was without a sense of self, without love.

Coño, she thought. How could she not have seen this as she had observed him?

Nereyda, I've never felt th—

Tengo novio, Nicanor.

Nereyda didn't know that her white lie would turn into poetry that would convert her into a traicionera. That he'd search for her love in the sky when all he needed was awareness of himself.

Papi

Papi's hands were thick and wide, perfect for slapping dough that would later turn into crust. They were perfect for pressing down the bottom of a mug into pieces of plantain to convert them into tostones. They were perfect for making the deep and sharp sounds of drums when he clapped in laughter to El Chapulin Colorado. They were perfect for tickling my sister and me at the same time until we laughed so hard we cried. His hands pretended to be the perfect tool for teaching Mami lessons.

Papi had a big and tender heart. It was perfect for feeling into people and really understanding them. It was perfect for loving all fifteen of his children. It was perfect for giving and giving to anyone who needed, to anyone who was short on their rent, to anyone who had to send money back to the island, to anyone who needed a vice to get by. Life was difficult, and money, when it came, was easy for Papi to make and give away. Papi's nickname was El Generoso.

Papi gave so much that sometimes he found himself without a thing, with no more to give, and Papi hit empty.

Papi was not raised to be empty. No matter how many times he found himself there, he did not learn how to handle himself within the constraints of zero. He did not know how to face it, and he sure could not do what Mami did: make a life out of nothing. So, when he was vacant, he filled himself with the pain of Mami and the fear that lived within my sister and me.

When Papi hit empty and he took to finding something to fill with, you could hear it in his voice. It grew lower and lower until there was a crash or a high-pitched yell. My big sister, who was only two years older than me, stood by always to see where she would have to rub menthol onto Mami later. Sometimes she tried to pull Papi off, but it only made it worse on Mami. We never talked about it because before we knew how to spell our names, we knew there were aspects of Papi we could not visit without hitting empty ourselves.

I always fled. I unlocked the front door and ran up to the attic of the building where no one would see me. I held my legs to my chest. I rocked and I prayed for Mami to be ok. My sister, she knew where to find me when Mami was asleep, when Papi stepped into the shower to wash off his sins. Papi would leave, but he'd always take one of us. Normally, I'd pretend to be asleep next to

Mami, so he would always take my sister. At first, I thought it was only fair because she watched so he had to fill her eyes with something other than the blows and the blood. But once, he took her, and we did not see her for the entirety of the summer. When he returned with her, she was quieter and prayed to Papa Dios y la Virgen and also lit candles to Los Misterios without being told to do so.

When I stood with Mami, I'd wait in silence for her to wake. Then, I'd let her do my hair without much complaining. I knew that it would keep her calm until she remembered my sister was gone. At that point she would shoo me off, tell me to go to the living room and do homework. I'd leave her, only to listen to her crying from the kitchen. Instead of practicing my math, I always made a list of all the things I loved about Papi and the one thing I hated about him. No matter how I added or subtracted the words on the paper, I knew I'd just rather be without a dad.

Cuero

Lauren

Lauren did not like habichuelas on her rice. She wanted them on her main plate, unlike her salad, but the grain had been set in a way that created a visual separation from the protein and the carb.

Set your own damn plate then, ¡malagradecida! Tired of this daily insistence, her mother, Lorena, yelled. Lorena even took to turning the plate around, slamming it to the ground, where it shattered right at her daughter's feet. Although Lorena had been born in Santo Domingo, she was raised in the Bronx too, and she wasn't like the other mothers in the neighborhood who served their kids out of guilt. Lauren cried while she held open a black plastic bag as her Abuela, Julia, swept and gathered the broken pieces.

Ya, ya, Lola, ya, everything will be alright, Julia cooed.

It was then Julia started cleaning up her granddaughter's messes and serving Lauren in a way she had never been able to serve Lorena. It was in the habit of separating la comida that she became hyper aware of the fact that her granddaughter did not appreciate the ways objects and particles found their way towards one another. She did not like the frenzy of mixed things. Lauren didn't talk to her grandmother much, not past a What did you do today? Did you talk to any of your friends? But Lauren chose to spend all her time in the living room with Julia and that was enough for the vieja. Amidst the hollering and fighting of *Caso Cerrado,* Julia often peered over Lauren's shoulder to discover her granddaughter could live with the mixing of symbols and letters.

Julia could not understand how much Lauren loved numbers. She herself had never been a scholar, and Lorena did not love anything past money. Lauren did math with letters, una matemáticas que Julia nunca aprendió en su país. Often when Lauren was at school, Julia went into her room and looked at the numbers. Lauren had entire marble notebooks filled with symbols and numbers and more symbols and numbers, and when Julia tried to really understand them, she felt her sanity slipping away. It was in one of these moments, seeking to understand, that a folded magazine poster of two naked women spread wide open and touching one another's exploding breasts

slipped out of it. After a, Santo Dios, Julia burned
it and never spoke of it again.

☾

Lauren was average. She knew it. And it
was something she held onto like a prize from God.
Unlike her mother, pregnant at fifteen, and her
grandmother, a teenage bride, she was ordinary.
She attributed the failures of the women who came
before her to their beauty and she knew beauty was
not what would stop her from achieving her goals.
Instead of losing herself to men, she was going to
lose herself to numbers, to codes, to girls who were
connected to the infinite. She was going to make it
out. Her offspring would not be raised in the Bronx
or en el barrio de donde salió su Abuela.

Best Friends For a Reason

Lauren invited her best friend, Michelle
María, over for dinner three times a week,
Mondays, Wednesdays, and Fridays. On Mondays,
they did the week's homework, on Wednesdays
they caught up on TV shows, and Fridays they went
to the salon to do their nails or their hair together.
It happened on a Friday.
They went home to drop off their bags, and Julia
had two plates out with the same components—
pollo asado, platanito verdes, and a green salad—
one was meticulously prepared for Lauren, and the

other was set to resemble a small mountain, like her own plate.

Michelle María had been coming over for three years, and Julia knew that the girl twirled the food on her plate and enjoyed mixing all the things together.

That's disgusting, Lauren told her best friend.

Pero, it's going to the same place, Michelle María responded, plus look at the colors. It's beautiful.

Julia loved Michelle María for many reasons, but mostly because the girl enjoyed having conversations with her. Michelle María asked questions, and in the answers, Julia received chances to pass down stories to her granddaughter and explain her shortcomings. Lauren pretended she didn't listen, but she'd put down her pencil, stop scribbling, and look her grandmother in the face.

On that Friday, Michelle María asked about Lauren's grandfather. Julia took a deep breath, picked up the bits of platanito verdes with the tips of her fingers.

Well, he—he did not believe in loving a woman as if she was his equal, his rib. He abused me, you know? Julia didn't want to detail the beatings, and the stealing of the small income she made at the postal office after she was knocked unconscious. And that's how we got here so fast Lorena and I, she added. My entire little barrio came together and decided that it was better to be in a place where it snowed than to be dead. Lauren picked up her pencil then.

So, basically, he was like my garbage sperm donor. It must run in the family, she mumbled. Michelle María peeked over her shoulder. Lauren was writing down an ASCII code.

The Coronas, the sneaked in sips of rum, and the chisme were the real reasons the young women made a habit of the salon. Lauren had wavy brown hair that she could do at home, and thus save the twenty-five dollars for the wash and set. Lorena told her that often but lost the argument the minute Lauren reminded her she could too and she didn't. Michelle María hated the pulling and tugging of her curly tresses. She had started dyeing it last year. On that Friday, it was blonde. The bleach had caused much more damage than she cared to admit.

The hairstylist, Denice, approached the both of them. Touched Lauren's hair and reminded her that some people would kill for the volume and thickness. Then she eyed Michelle María and mentioned something she just had to try, like a leave in or a treatment. This time it was a Brazilian Keratin treatment.

What does it do? Michelle María wanted to know. Tugging on her brittle baby hairs Denice responded that it would kill the stiffness in her hair. Michelle María looked in the mirror. The dark brown of her skin made her feel dusty and like she was trying too hard after Denice had touched her.

Why do you always tell me nice things about my hair, but you never say anything nice to Michelle María? Lauren stepped in.

Porque lo tuyo es natural, take the compliment and sit down, Denice rolled her eyes and laughed into the mirror with the other hairstylists, all in tight jeans and heels.

You all just hate yourselves, you know? Lauren yelled. The clientele sipped their Coronas, pretended to read a magazine, or watched Lauren be ignored. Fuck this, Lauren said, let's go. Michelle María's eyes watered and the embarrassment pushed red out of all that brown.

The freezing temperatures calmed the turmoil and the heat on their skin. Thank you, Michelle María said, when they stood at the bus stop waiting for the one bus. Lauren placed her hood over her head and then she brought Michelle Maria's on for her.

Don't say thank you, Lauren responded. She opened her arms and Michelle María plunged into her. Lauren took in the scent of the fresh ocean—it was what Michelle María's Dolce & Gabbana perfume reminded her of. As Michelle María pulled away from the embrace, Lauren leaned her forehead onto Michelle María's. What she wouldn't give to let Michelle María view herself from her eyes? She had never seen another human carry the world with grace like Michelle María did. Michelle María exhaled and created a small cloud of fog around her face. She tried to wipe away her tears, but Lauren licked them playfully.

You're a clown, Michelle María laughed.
Lauren wasn't laughing. She was dead serious.
She wanted to taste the ocean within her best
friend. She closed in the gap between the bridges
of their noses. Waves of anxiety sunk from her
chest into her stomach. Michelle María smirked
and the pressure departed. Lauren touched her
best friend's cheek, leaned in, and kissed her best
friend. Not bothered by her lips, Michelle María
kissed Lauren back. Lauren felt an upsurge
between her thighs, and she swore to herself she
wouldn't pull back, not even to breathe. The ardor
their bodies created underneath their bubble coats
was enough to withstand the cold. Their tongues
wavered in one another's mouth searching for
anything other than the truth at hand. Lauren
sucked on Michelle María's lips and she didn't pull
away. This, Lauren was sure, this was it.

The booming horn from a Hummer was
what forced their bodies to peel from one another.

Vamos a ver par de patas, let's be friends. I
promise it'll set you right, the driver winked at
them.

Michelle María

Michelle María did not see the art in
matching, curating, or keeping it all in a single
palette. Although her school had a uniform policy,
her socks, leggings, and headband, always said
something. On weekends, she adorned her body
with playful patterns, textures, and colors. When
her mother packed boxes to send back to the island,

she pushed them up into her room and went through each item picking out the things she knew she could bring back. In these boxes, she had found her mother's cheetah print leggings and a lilac jumpsuit from the late '80s.

¡Esto es lo último¡ When her mother walked in she was scavenging another box that had yet to be sealed. Michelle María's mother had clearly heard about the situation en el Salon de Denice. I told you not to do esa mierda to your hair, and now you're going to embarrass me with clientele? Gloria yelled. Michelle did not open her mouth. Instead, she went into her head and bought together words to ease the tension that gathered in her jaw in the shape of a colín:

> *Mujer de mil hombres,*
> *Mujer sin nombre,*
> *I wish, woman, I could tell you*
> *I don't see you as a mother.*
> *You are my foe.*
> *You are a trifling ho—*

Gloria's manoplazo landed like a boulder on the side of Michelle María's face. Pay attention, Michelle María! No me vuelva a ser pasar una maldita vergüenza asi, malcriada de mierda. Gloria stared down at her daughter as if she wanted to fight her, like Michelle María had stopped her from something bigger than numbers. Michelle María calculated her breath, determined not to give her mother the war she wanted.

Thankfully, the phone rang, and Michelle María watched her mother strut out of the living room. Her ass was perfect since she had gotten the lipo and a Brazilian buttlift. Michelle María could not stand that the process had just made her mother more comparona.

Gloria ran numbers. Numbers in the hottest bodegas, salons, and barbershops in four boroughs. Michelle María didn't like the numbers game, but she knew that it was all her mother was good at. Her mother was loud. So loud you'd think she was still in the campo speaking from the inside of her house to someone on the outer edge of her fence. Michelle María did not talk at home or next to her mother, so for all her mother knew, she was a silent girl. Michelle María was embarrassed by Gloria, and if she could avoid bringing her to a parent-teacher conference or outings with any other adults, she would. There was no point, Michelle María thought. Gloria always had a Bluetooth stuck to her ear as if she was a mayor and she found herself excusing herself three times within a five-minute conversation.

Michelle María hated numbers because they had turned her mother into a cold machine; all she cared about was el dinero. When Lauren tried to explain the beauty of numbers, Michelle María said numbers were the white man's thing. Numbers is how they fucked us up, Lauren, trust me. Michelle María threw herself at words instead. She danced with them, she wept with them, she slept with them, she breathed with them. When she allowed boys and men into her room during her mother's absence, she loved with words. She traced poetry onto their sweaty backs knowing that the pain, the shame, the guilt, the tension of being her would bring more words to create collisions with.

Después de la pela de lengua, Gloria ventured out of the house and Michelle María called Dante. Dante was twenty-two, he was a senior when she was a freshman, and now he went to Hostos College and studied nutrition. His back and his arms would tell you he followed his nutrition plans to a T, but his abs competed with a round pouch from the beers he chugged. He still undressed the minute he got into the door like he had nothing to hide. She never took off her shirt, and only took off her pants because he massaged the knots out her cheeks and took care of her before he took care of him.

When they had gone at it for four rounds, and she held her tongue instead of reminding him he had to go, her mother was coming in an hour, she felt the words fly through her head.

Next time,
with my tongue,
I will paint a garden
from your toes to your face.
The sun will shine from your chest
to nurture the plants we make;
all the time,
I will water them.

My favorite fruits exist below your hips.
Don't they?

48

What did you write this time? He lethargically opened his eyes.

Nunya, she teased. Usually she shared, but today she did not know if the words were for him.

Words and Michelle María were a match made for the ages. Most of the time, they clicked.

Lauren Eats

The Kiss was never mentioned; Lauren did not want to ruin her chances and Michelle María believed that if something was not spoken about, it didn't happen. When Michelle María went away for college things changed slowly and in a haze. Still, there were the occasional texts and conversation on the phone when pain erupted from either of them. When the angst of higher education became too much, they could only lean on each other because only they knew where they had come from.

On various occasions, Michelle María called Lauren to tell her about the racism and colorism on campus. At first it was to talk out frustrations about what Lauren considered to be little things; remarks white kids made about the Bronx and Michelle María's accent or how white girls asked Michelle María how she got her hair to disobey gravity? Michelle María hated that when white people asked questions in class regarding any group of color, she was looked at for answers. But what she hated more was the case she sometimes found herself making for their ignorance. Soon enough the calls became about wider issues Lauren believed had nothing to do with her best friend like the case of students wearing blackface to a Halloween party. Although Lauren had never paid enough attention to gringos to see them out of character, she sighed and tried to be supportive. But Michelle María wouldn't let it go. Weeks after her venting session about the blackface, she sent Lauren a newspaper article that exposed the fraternity house who had organized the Blackface event. Can you believe this shit? I swear they have no respect, she texted.

Lauren called her then, tried to coach her through solutions. Maybe you can start a petition to have them expelled or wear white face and see if it bothers them, she offered.

Es que me tienen jarta, Michelle María ignored Lauren. I just don't understand why people of color always have to be the bigger people when it comes to shit like this. Like we have to be understanding that you think our fucking skin is a costume prop? Fuck! Sometimes I just want to leave this place, you know?

You're lucky to be there, Michelle María, Lauren finally said. Just get your four years done and be through with it. It isn't like they're killing people on campus.

(

For MLK weekend during their second semester of their sophomore year in college, Michelle María invited Lauren to visit her campus.

She invited her up instead of going down because
Michelle María was scared. Scared that the Bronx
would swallow her and keep her the way it had
kept a number of students from The City she had
crossed paths with. Lauren obliged and boarded a
bus on a Thursday night. Lorena encouraged her
to have fun, to drink illegally, to let her hair down;
since Michelle María left, Lauren spent all her time
coding. Julia sneaked in a crucifix into her duffle
bags.

On the first night, they went to a friend's
dorm room. Carolina's dorm was where everyone
went to pregame before they hit Neal's, an
off-campus bar known to let students in. Lauren
liked bubbly things. Michelle María had already
acquired a taste for the burn that moved down her
throat into her stomach like a stone.

Shots, shots, shots.

Carolina's boyfriend came by with his
friends. Lauren watched Michelle María's face
flush and fall, and so she held her hand.

You ok? She whispered into her ear.
Michelle María smiled and nodded.

I fuck him, she said, when I'm bored.
Lauren raised an eyebrow and swallowed the sour
taste in her mouth. Michelle María was her
mother's daughter, yet she always provided
details, always told her about new guys.

His name was Isaiah, and he was on the
basketball team. His calves were strong with
muscle, and his forearms filled with vascularity.
Lauren knew this was Michelle María's type. She
watched him leaning off of the armchair and

whispering into her ear. Michelle María giggled, covering her mouth like she had something to hide. The words had not been coming to her lately, and so she wanted something to happen with Isaiah, something past their nights watching Netflix on his bed and then fucking until their alarm clocks reminded them to get up for class.

Lauren chugged her Bacardi Breezer. The Kiss and the times she slept over after it, fighting herself crazy to avoid touching Michelle María's skin awake, rushed into her. She approached them, carelessly disrupting the intimate laughter.

When we heading out? she asked. Michelle María stood up swiftly and moved away from Isaiah and closer to Lauren. We can go now, she said.

Ayyyeee, ya ready? Isaiah shouted although the dorm room was small, and the music was not loud at all. All his boys nodded, moved away from the beer pong table that had sprouted between twin sized beds. I didn't know they were coming, Michelle María whispered to Lauren on their way out. Her heart fluttered, her palms grew sweaty.

Blanquito's Bar is what the group nicknamed Neal's. The girls in the group warned Lauren that there was not much to admire unless she was into white guys, which she wasn't. They weren't exaggerating either, the rock music could be heard from a block away. When they entered Isaiah went straight to the DJ, who plugged in his phone to some J.Cole. Lauren looked around at the dark wood furniture and the neon green lights behind the bar. Every wall was covered with posters, no blank space for Lauren to paint numbers with her eyes. The drinks started coming in quickly, faster than Lauren expected, so when they touched her hand, she didn't have an option to say she did not drink anything that wasn't bubbly and sweet. She just drank, squinting her eyes and then sucking in her cheeks in disgust.

Mostly she watched as Michelle María bent over to trap songs and shook the things Lauren wished she could put in her mouth. Michelle María was different here. Her hair was healthier, her dark coils jumped with her. Her skirt hugged her hips. And even though nothing she said sounded like poetry anymore, she seemed to have found something Lauren could not quite name. Lauren walked towards her. Reaching her she said, Come with me to the bathroom.

After they both used the bathroom, Michelle María tied up her gold satin shirt and kissed Lauren's cheek before running back out to dance. As she followed her best friend, Lauren could not remember how many drinks they had, so she started her attempt to retrace her memory. On her fingers.

One. When they first got in, a shot right after, and another. Three. Then Michelle María didn't like her drink, it was too sweet she had said, and Lauren had it for her. Four. Then another shot with Carolina. Five. And another shot out of Michelle María's belly button.

Six.

She had had six drinks since she had been at the bar. How many hours had it been? She looked up to realize she had lost Michelle María. The room twirled around her—she did not yet know how to drink.

From where Lauren stood, she could see Isaiah's head, and so she walked towards him, bumping into limbs and the cool sweat of strangers. Glass shattered. Laughter. Shot. Shot. Shot. By the time she got to him, Lauren did not see Michelle María's face, she saw him. Grabbing Michelle María's ass through her skirt like it was his. It scrunched up in his hands like it had found the perfect grip to reside in. He kissed her forehead as if he had everything to protect her. Their eyes met, and he whispered something into Michelle María's ear that made her turn around and head towards Lauren.

Why him? Lauren yelled above the music. Michelle María was confused.

Here, drink water, she responded twisting off the cap off of her water bottle. She brought it to Lauren's lips, and Lauren sucked the bottle dry.

How many poems have you written for him? Lauren yelled. Michelle María ignored her, the alcohol now hitting her as well. Tell me, she yelled. But Michelle María had nothing to tell. You're just like my mother, you're just like yours, too, Lauren screamed. Lauren turned to give her back to Michelle María, but her stomach spiraled like an albuca spiralis, and she vomited on the floor and at the feet of others.

Alright, you have to go, kid, a tall, pale security guard grabbed Lauren by the elbow. Michelle María followed yelling at the security

guard to get off her friend until she ended up
slipping on the vomit. Isaiah helped her get up,
and she pushed him off, ran after Lauren who was
throwing up into the vent of a house.

☾

Once in the dorm room, Michelle María's
struggle to get Lauren into the bathroom rushed
the alcohol right through her liver and she felt alert.
Lauren could not pick up her head from her chest.
In the shared bathrooms, Michelle María undressed
herself and then undressed Lauren paying little
attention to the softness of her skin. They both put
their bare feet into one of the showers. Michelle
María washed her back with a loofah while Lauren
cried. Lauren had only ever seen the infinite in
numbers and now she trembled at the fear to see it
in the flesh. So, she glued her eyes to Michelle
María's feet, wet with water, to avoid breaking her
own heart again. She wanted to look up, to see the
curve and the indentations on her best friend's
body, but it hurt. To touch all the parts on Michelle
María's body would propel her into a boundless
emotion and then she'd have to lose her. She
sobbed at the possibility.
I'm starving, Lauren said, as Michelle María
tucked her into her bed. Her own stomach also
growled. I can walk to the 711, she said, they have
pizza and snacks and stuff. Lauren nodded. That
would have to be good enough.
Lauren chugged the bottled water Michelle
María left by the bed and paged through a book she

found under the bed. Bored with words, she put the book down, turned on her stomach, and decided to start finding herself. A knock at the door disrupted her. She walked to the door, wrapping the robe that smelled just like the ocean, around her.

Who? She asked.

Isaiah.

What do you want? She opened the door.

Michelle María? He looked inside the small room.

She's not here, Lauren said. When he walked into the room after announcing he'd wait, Lauren asked, Jesus, how comfortable are you with each other? He ignored her, sat on the empty bed, and took out his phone.

Lauren paged through the book.
She paged through the book.
She paged through the book.

She reached for his thigh and then convinced herself to reach higher before she changed her mind. Isiah dropped his phone and smirked. She ran her hand up and down and down and up.

She rubbed and he shook his head. Stop, he said, I really like Michelle María. She added pressure to her touch.

It looks like you like me too. She kneeled down in front of him. He opened his mouth to protest. It's ok, she said as she moved him to her lips. The hardness filled the spaces in her mouth.

56

Her body went empty and blank. At least I know I'm not into men at all, she thought.

Take off her robe, he whispered in an angry moan, it's not yours take it off. She took off the robe exposing her thinness, him still in her.

I don't even like white girls man, he laughed sadly. And yet he still placed his hand over her head, prompting her to continue. When she gagged, he took sharp breaths and told her to keep going. His encouragement empowered, disgusted, and delighted her.

Honey, I'm home. I've got— Michelle María opened the door.

Between the movement and the heavy breathing Isaiah and Lauren had failed to hear the sucking of the key card.

What the fuck, Lauren? Michelle María yelled throwing the snacks on the floor. What the fuck, yo? The pain knocked the wind out her lungs.

Isaiah pushed Lauren off and quickly pulled up his pants. Gloria had taught Michelle María that men were going to do as they did, so it was seeing Lauren on her knees that rushed anguish into her guts. It was knowing that this was it.

Why?!

Lauren hurried to put the robe back on. Isaiah tried to approach her. It didn't mean nothing, it was nothing, he repeated.

Get the fuck out, she yelled. Although he begged to be heard, he left without much fight. Michelle María pushed Lauren into her bed, tears in her eyes making everything a blur. Why, Lauren? Why would you do this to me?

Lauren knew the world would not end for either of them, but she also had never seen hungry fury in her friend. She sat up on Michelle María's twin sized bed with her knees to her chin waiting for the blows or for whatever Michelle María was willing to deliver.

When Michelle María's sobs subsided, Lauren looked over into the corner she had crawled into. The problem is you are just like our mothers—gullible—Michelle María, so I had to show you that men are trash. They really ain't shit. We're the ones. We hold the infinite.

Michelle María squinted her eyes and shook her head. She could not form the words to have Lauren understand that this was not about men because maybe it was. Maybe this was her karma for saying Isaiah was someone for boredom. He was not. He was someone Michelle María had found to fill in the loneliness, and he had filled more than that. Michelle María had lied to Lauren, and now she wanted to rip out her own tongue. She sobbed, curled up in fetus on her roommate's bed. Although her rage told her to kick Lauren out at the moment, she was not going to. She picked herself up, propping herself up with her hands. She coughed and willed the words to express the anger and the hurt.

You must be happy, finally you realize you're fucking universal. A heartless cuero like the rest of us after all, huh?

Seventeen, Lauren whispered.

What?

You've fucked around with seventeen guys.

What is it to you? IT'S MY PUSSY, bitch! I do with it what I want. I give it to who I choose. It's not yours, Michelle María yelled.

What is it to you then that I sucked one of them off? Lauren whispered. Michelle Maria tilted her head in disbelief. You are such a fucking ruthless ass bitch, you know that? What has happened to you?

You, Lauren replied, You have fucking happened to me.

Oh my god! She rolled her eyes. You're fucking crazy. It was one kiss.

To you, Michelle María, it was just a kiss but to me it was The Kiss. It meant something to me because I am not at the level of maldita cuero you're on!

The silence was loud enough to hear the crickets outside the window and the squeaking of the bed above them.

Get the fuck out of my room the minute the sun comes up, Michelle María growled.

El Alto Manhattan

It was in the apparent heat developed between spring and summer, that they spotted each other.

Michelle María was walking down the Dyckman strip about to meet a friend from college for brunch. She wore yellow and orange on her top and black bottoms with patent leather black heels.

Although college was three years ago, it seemed like a lifetime ago. Michelle María was excited to show that she was up to something. Her collection of poetry was a hit, and people from all over the country and Caribbean reached out to her to express their gratitude and to share that they saw themselves on the pages of her collection. She had finally found the way to tap into words without the pain. Her curls made a monumental halo around her head.

Lauren stopped at the light. Pressed down on the horn to her Honda Civic when she realized it was her. Honked again when Michelle María continued to strut across the street. And then Lauren rolled down the window to the passenger's seat. Mamá, llamela, she requested.

Julia stuck her head out the window. Michelle María! ¡Soy yo! Mira—over here! And Michelle María looked back. Her chest contracted when she turned around to see Lauren and the woman who had fed her on the days her mother failed to set a plate. Smiling widely, she waved.

¡Que dios te bendiga, mi'ja! Julia yelled out the window remembering the way this child had seen her, remembering the ways she had forced her granddaughter to acknowledge her stories.

The pressure of Lauren's beating heart pressed up against the highest edge of her mouth. She crouched as best as she could in the driver's seat to ensure Michelle María could see her waving. Michelle María pressed her lips and acknowledged Lauren with an upward tilt of her chin. The light changed from green to red. Lauren watched her turn around and go. If it weren't for the honking behind her, she would've watched her walk away until she disappeared.

You never really said what happened with you two? Julia stated rolling up the window.

I liked my rice white, my beans separated, and my salad in a different bowl, and she did not, Lauren smiled.

Julia appreciated that the friendship had left her granddaughter with more words than she had before in her arsenal. Still, she wondered when her granddaughter would find the words to free herself and whether or not she'd be prepared.

Justice

No one comes to this city to live or to love.

Until just recently our building's entrance
has been given a fresh coat of paint, the entrance
has been decorated with antique rugs, Avant-Garde
light fixtures have been installed, and a surplus of
natural plants have sprouted—as if five years ago
the lungs of my people were not capable of turning
oxygen to carbon dioxide. The newcomers still find
aspects of this city to complain about; Starbucks are
too crowded, restaurants have no Wifi, people talk
too fast, mornings are tense, sound systems have
too much base. We can't make them comfortable
and still be us, but we manage.

The buildings that stand in the place of
those that once burned down surround the bridge
and watch. The sky is darkening. Yet, the sun
floats in that middle space where it teases us
humans with its proximity before leaving.

The bricks of the buildings resemble roasted cacao beans—a dark red leaning towards maroon.

Sometimes I be wishing that the buildings didn't have inhabitants, that like in China's desert cities there was no one to watch. It's just I'd like privacy outside sometimes, but that's not something we are awarded around these parts.

Once upon a time, Mami herself was a pair of eyes, a watcher, from our fifth-floor walk-up. She'd sit at the window with a Marlboro short y una taza de café watching, clocking people who had the time she would not be granted. She claimed she wasn't like the other people who watched, I watch, pero I don't entertain bochinche or spread anybody's business. What they do in these streets is on them. On one of her last days, she choked on the smoke she was trying to blow, smudged her red lipstick as she covered her mouth through the cough. When I tried to help her to the living room she pushed me off, relájate, muchacha. She went back to the window and adjusted her leopard print frames on the bridge of her wide nose. ¿Mueble pa' que? She said, si todavía me queda tiempo pa' mirar.

His vomit is thin and warm in between my toes.

All I want is to give you everything, he says. He brushes the back of his hand on the side of his mouth. The cars flash by, cutting the boroughs with speed. People walk around us, breaking their necks to look back. No one takes a moment to sit on the fact that they are in two places at once.

Did you hear me? He wraps his palm around the left side of his neck like a vine. I am no longer surprised by the comfort he takes in the ways he releases himself on me; instead, it alleviates me since it grants the bitterness inside of me a reason to exist.

Today, he had arrived from the hospital with a number. The verbal abuse he received during the sixteen-hour shift from the white doctors didn't matter for the first time in a month. He had finally been given a number. I was working on my research when he kissed my back. I turned away from the books to face him and he whispered, I can take care of us now.

For the last three years, we have lived off of our savings (mostly my own), and my part time job at the writing center, so that he could finish medical school, and I could try to finish graduate school. $67,000. Full benefits. I kissed his forehead trying to alleviate him from the pressure to provide. He carried me over to the bed. An hour later, I sat on his back picking at ingrown hairs. Let's cross the bridge and find a nice place to celebrate, he suggested. I wore sandals and a sundress. We got on each other again before leaving. The bitterness nowhere to be found.

The bitterness had appeared on a random day. Honest to God. His head was on my lap while we watched *El Patron Del Mal*. He read the subtitles and said, They just need to catch this fat fuck already. And there it was: the bitterness, a seed in my stomach. Pablo Escobar was a criminal, he was responsible for deaths and addiction, so why the hell was I so defensive? Two days later, the seed of bitterness germinated when I had to bribe him to wash the dishes since I had cooked. And then the bitterness grew that night when he claimed he deserved me for washing them.

My therapist asked me to begin a list every time I felt bitter. At first it was a tiny list. Recently, it had sprouted. Different branches appeared every time he came home. Different leaves every time he asked me about his pills, about what was for dinner, about my plans for the day. Different roots every time he started a sentence with, Oh, if you could.

The vomit is violet from wine. I stare at it all up in between my toes as I begin to walk.

I did, I say placing his book bag on my shoulder. He walks alongside me with his hand on my right shoulder. He squeezes, waiting for an answer. Well, you can't, I say almost in a whisper.

Why not? He asks. Why can't I give you that? I am left taking the next two steps alone.

My mother didn't teach me dependency, I want to yell and enunciate. I cannot force myself to need you. Mami taught me to use my tongue like a sword, and I haven't sharpened it in years. Too afraid, I find myself, to pain him, to say things that might strike him the wrong way. Some feelings just don't translate. He complains about that. He claims he wants to hear me say the things I want to say. Yet when I begin to say them, he finds ways to bring it back to me, and my list grows. If I say I want to attract structure into my career, he talks about my home habits. If I say I want more clarity on a project, he says I should start creating SMART goals and clearing out the apartment; he doesn't seem to get that papers pile up because I have to process, that laundry gets left for last because I have to balance both of our struggles to survive. Sometimes I don't know what it is I am doing with my life, but I do know what I am doing for his. Day in and day out I desire to tell him these things. But language is a thing my mother gave to me to defend and to destroy.

Terrible things have happened to me. You know that, he says. And the bitterness returns, a root opens up a route inside my stomach. I am heavy, and I want to find the machete in me. To swing it like a baseball bat and rid myself of the bitterness. I try to pinpoint the feeling. My back.

You have been through terrible things, I begin. But it could be worse. The sun lowers into the water under the bridge. He claims I am minimizing his pain. I try to explain that things could be worse. He has food, shelter, clothes on his back, people that love him, his dream job. He has me. I bite my tongue. I want to continue, tell him we all have to get by. You never hear me complaining. When the cancer conquered my mother's body, I only knew she was in pain because in her dreams she couldn't keep herself from talking. I never heard her complain during the day.

Let me try to take care of you, he says again. I shake my head.

Why?! He yells. Let me take a guess, he rubs his goatee. Is it because I'm buried in $250,000 deep? Cause I can't afford an apartment on my own? Cause I don't like the way you cook your damn chicken? Cause the way I like to fuck you hurts? Cause you secretly wish I was lighter so your Papi can applaud? Tell me. Go on say it, let me hear it.

This everlasting tail of questions I've heard before. I have never taken the time to construct a response. I turn and begin to walk away from him. With a free shoulder again, my back forces me to bring back equilibrium.

☾

The week we met he introduced me to his cousin, who he shared his Harlem apartment with. He held my elbow from the door and led me into the kitchen.

Look man, she no nigger. Isn't she beautiful?

I clenched my teeth into a wide smile as I digested his words. Felt the same lips my cousins nicknamed cocola bembes spread across my face.

Elidania, I said shaking his hand. If you must open up with my race, babe, Black or Afro-Latina is good with me.

They laughed. You not Black at all, his cousin scoffed. He returned to sipping ginger ale out of a thick plastic cup.

I am, I whispered.

Where? He turned around with the answer of an assumption on his eyelids.

I don't have to give you a history lesson on the island I come from. But here's my grandfather—if the proof ain't pigmented enough for you on my skin, I said pulling out my phone and searching for the picture of us en la finca. My grandfather shines under the sun. In the picture, I am a piece of lace curved around his lower body. I turned my phone to them feeling dumb for trying to prove something that didn't need to be.

How'd that happen? He asked looking at the same skin on my bones Papi calls me Negra for, the same layer my grandfather took pride over since all my cousins had taken after their light skinned fathers instead of leaning on him.

Justice, I responded meaning every syllable. Abuela still tells the stories even when her Parkinson's is at its worst. Her father a general, my grandfather in charge of tending his lands. The war my grandparents had to declare, the things they had to give up, the times they almost met death, to finally be together. When my mother was conceived, they claimed it felt like justice to both sides.

They laughed so loud and wide that I thought the edges of their mouths would rip.

Let me tell you about justice, girl, his cousin cleared his throat obnoxiously. My great, great grandma was what white folks liked to call a mammy, and they locked her in a barn with my great, great grandpops. They made my great grandmomma big, black, and bold. My great grandmomma grew up and got her a light skin brother. When my grandmomma decided to lay with another dark-skinned nigga, she couldn't stand looking at her own children. So, you just imagine her rage when my moms ended up doing the same shit she done did. She tried everything to get my moms to abort—pushed her down some stairs, kicked her in her sleep. I'm surprised the crazy bitch didn't try to poison her. But when I came out looking like her daddy, a little light skin and shit, she looked at my moms and said, Justice.

The waves of laughter they shared nauseated me, and I swallowed.

So, you ain't Black none, he declared. I should've run out from that mess right then and there is what my homegirls been telling me. But the myth I made in my head is that love could set into motion the progression of individual men.

☾

I don't want you to give me everything. Your main goal shouldn't be to give me everything. It doesn't make me happy, ok? I say. I make sure my voice rings with conviction. I make sure to say it loud for him to hear behind me.

I keep walking, dragging my sandals, the sweat from the night's heat gather under my armpits and at the scoop of my back. I stop and turn to him—tired.

You know what I want? I feel the blood rush to the outermost edges of my vessels. You've gotten so good at feeling your pain, talking about your trauma that you've forgotten ALL of us have our own shit. What I'd love from you is for you to shut the fuck up and listen once in a while. That's all. That don't cost you nothing. I continue to walk across the bridge.

Tonight's dinner was filled with wine and multiple courses. $287. The most lavish meal we'd had our entire relationship. Throughout the laughter I concluded, tonight would be a good night. I should've remembered that every minute is a new day with him.

The first time I saw him, his skin popped from the collar and the cuffs of his suit as he waited to cross avenues. I tried to look away, but his skin was dark silk. I wanted his skin in between my fingers. I tried to look away remembering that I was in a rush to get to class, that I didn't have time. But he was a galaxy, and I gravitated to him. I stood beside him waiting for the light to change. As we crossed the street, he looked over at me, and I said, Hi.

Two months later, he moved into my place. My father failed at his attempt to hide his disgust at my birthday dinner.

Un fokin' prieto, Papi whispered that night. If your mother were alive, te comería viva. Knowing damn well she would've directed him to the nearest mirror.

He'll be out in a month when he starts beating her, my Madrina told my cousins, and when they said nothing, she added ¿Quien sabe? She might be into that, too.

It was during month number three that I came to terms with the fact that my life had become a black hole. I'd never leave without havoc.

You know what, I say. I attempt to stuff down all I've said inside of me. Come on. Let's just make it home. I'll give you a massage, and you can take your pills.

Silence. Silence.

I've been praying for a number to make him feel whole, and still, he had something to go on about. God, have you been listening at all? My feet stop, I let my head go— heavy from the wine, heavy from caretaking, heavy from loving a man that will strive to become a man I don't want, a man he cannot ever be. He came to this city to flower, considered me the soil. His parents secretly sent money to a PO Box every few months— thankful that I'd managed to love a child they had fought themselves on loving for twenty-seven years.

Silence still.

Come o—, I begin to moan turning around. His legs drape the railings of the bridge. The Harlem River is calm underneath. I drop the messenger bag and run. Run because I'm not ready to focus on myself. Run because I need someone to take care of. Run because I don't want silence— God, listen—I don't want silence! Please.

All I want is to give you everything, girl, he looks at me as he continues to look out into the river, Why can't you believe that's a good thing?

You're right. I want you to give me everything, baby. Get off and give it to me. Come on.

You don't understand any of this, he says.

I don't, I cry. Teach me, show me.

The blue and red lights assault our eyes. I beg him to get off before the cops do what they do. The door to the car opens and closes and the cop moves forward until his body is a shadow on the pavement next to mine. He clears his throat.

Sir, I'm going to need you to step down. Desmond chuckles. Or what man? You gon' shoot me?

I look at the cop. He could be Italian or Puerto Rican; there's no difference between them anymore. Still, I hope it's the latter. I hope he grew up in a place like this one. That he once had a friend the color of Desmond. It might mean nothing or it might mean everything in this second.

No man, I'm not trying to have you be another brother in a casket. Please make your way down, and we won't even file this. I eye the cop. I don't trust it, but I hope it works. I don't have the funds for a funeral. I don't have the words for delivery or speeches or retelling.

Now that I'm talking to you from this position, Mr. Officer, can you tell me one thing? He stands, widens his stance, crosses his arms. His balance impeccable. The cop nods. Signals to his partner in the car to stand down.

What you think about my girl? You think she Black?

Yeah, yeah, why not? He responds looking me up and down. How does she love you?

Hard. Real hard, Desmond shakes his head. To be honest like my mother never did.

He looks at me, and I turn my head because it would not be of no use for him to see the shame spread across my face. I don't care anymore, he can just jump. The bitterness nauseates me. My liver has processed the wine, so I know what I mean, and I mean what I say.

But I'm a crazy nigga. That's what people been thinking since I've been on meds since I was eight. I just got lucky my pops wanted me to be a quarterback. You know, I got the build for it, but I've also got a good memory—photographic one. My grandpops talked to one of his fraternity brothers into guiding me into medicine, he says. You wanna hear this, right? Desmond doesn't wait for the cop to answer and continues. Well, the truth is he didn't want my come up to be about entertaining the white man or what not, but other people say it's cause he thought it more respectable. Either way, as of last month, man, I'm officially a DOCTOR can you believe that shit? And I keep trying to figure out how I'm going to help others live when, on some serious shit, my head is always halfway out the game.

The moon cares not to see this spectacle. His eyes glisten in the dark. He is a star. A star in the middle of his full-blown episode.

If your woman loves you despite the thoughts you're having, the officer looks at me, then she seems like a strong Black woman to me. I scoff. That's what they do, don't they? His eyes meet mine. Come on, you know that's what ya do.

Well then, I can't, Desmond's voice cracks. He claims he cannot continue to fuck up the legacy of Black women. His head drops between his shoulders and I've never seen him be so small.

Brother, the officer rubs his hands together,
how about you listen to my story for a bit?
Desmond lifts his head and looks out towards the
buildings across the river. His stance symmetrical
all the way through as if he is not standing between
life and death.

My lady put up with a bunch of shit from
me while I was in the academy. All my
frustrations, she paid for them. I've made it my
life's mission to repair that. It's not easy, but we
have moments. You think leaving this young
woman to have moments on her own is the
answer?

Baby go get everything you deserve. He
opens his arms, and I leap for his foot. Other than
the ruffling sounds his body makes against gravity
as he falls, there is no screaming or yelling from
him as if he's jumped bridges thousands of times
before. Like he's well aware of heights and the
depth of waters.

I run from the bridge. Soon, my sandals
come off. I run. The pavement is warm on the soles
of my bare feet. I run, I run.

Run.

Run.

Run.

The cop rolls down his window when he
approaches the curb I'm resting on. Desmond was

pulled out of the water. He suffered a concussion, but he'll be just fine, he says. The sweat pours down my face and hangs off my nose and the curve of my lip. The underbelly of my dress is soaked. As I catch my breath, I shake my head and watch the fluid from me darken the pavement.

Even if he suffered no injuries, our limbs won't ever work the same. Despite everything I have done, all the calculated moves to keep us afloat, none of us are content. It doesn't work.

I cannot hold together something that wants to break, I whisper into my chest. In the past, I've cried, but tonight I wail. The ache. The ache at the bottom of my back, the tug at my heart, the complexion of my arms—if I am Black and woman, I'm tired of it. If I am a reflection of God, where is the glory?

¡Oye! a man yells from his second-floor window. On reflex, I look up. He blows a kiss, waves for me to come up. I take a deep breath, give him the finger, and get into the cop's car.

☾

No one comes to this city to live or love. If I was born and bred here, of what purpose am I?

☾

The music is going and the fire hydrants are still open by the time I get back to my block. People sit by the entrance of the buildings with hookahs and white styrofoam cups. Grown men sit on coolers, while the women lay back in beach chairs with cup holders.

I gave the account to the precinct and called his parents. After they arrived, they told me to go home. They smirked uncomfortably, took deep breaths, and looked at me as if they knew this day would come. As if they knew from the start that I did not have it in me.

Morena, ¿todo bien? El Super looks at my bare feet as I put the key into the door. I nod.

Excuse me! A white woman in her early thirties catches up to me. We haven't met, she says, I'm Helen. I moved here three weeks ago. Would you please be able to translate? She looks at El Super.

What you gotta say? I let the door go.

Please, she catches her breath. Listen, I admire the unity of the people in this building. But it's 11:45 pm, I get up at seven a.m. tomorrow for work. Some of us, we are just trying to get some sleep. Can you please let him know that? El Super and I look at each other.

He understands, I reply rolling my eyes.

You speak to me before, Ms. Smithson, he says. Why you now think I know no English?

Helen says she's told him about the noise at this hour, but nothing has changed. She just thought that maybe her words weren't being received correctly. El Super laughs. She laughs irritably.

You got three ¿Come que se dice? Ehh, choices, Mami, El Super begins. He brings out his pinky finger, You can stay, have a good time. It's summertime! My son can teach you how to dance bachata for free. My people, we love the hot and we love the music loud it touches us in here, he says as he points to his chest. All winter we inside like rats. Is not natural for us, you know? So, summertime means this. He opens his arms wide framing the background.

The fire hydrant pumps out water in all its glory. A teenage boy uses a plastic bag to funnel the water pressure. Kids run through in wet oversized t-shirts. Men are gathered around the domino table, some of their children stand over their shoulders, learning. Women lay back on white plastic chairs, laughing, weightless, their feet up on sweating coolers. She stares at him blankly.

You no understand? he asks, Why waste the two little months la naturaleza give to us here? Helen opens her mouth to interject. He waves his left ring finger at her.

Number two, he begins. The first third of his finger is missing. Mami once told me it was from his days in the bodega. Díque he was slicing deli meat on the machine, and he started talking to his partner, and BAM!

Helen, ear plugs, he says like he's discovered something great for her. I chuckle. From Walgreens or Duane Reade—whatever you want—but Walgreens is lower prices, and it's twenty-four hours, you know? he exclaims. You want me to send a niño to get for you? He takes out a crumpled five-dollar bill from his pocket and whistles. Victor ven acá hazme el favor— ame un mandao real quick. Victor crosses the street standing on the right pedal of his bicycle.

No, no, Helen says. She crosses her arms over her chest. The blonde hairs on her arms standing.

Ok, three, El Super now has his pinky, ⅔ of his ring finger, and his middle finger out. If you don't like this, you can take all your nice things. All the things I helped you put together from IKEA with no tip, you can take all those things and, he twists his hands together. You can break them, put them back into the box, and you can go. No problem. No worries. I help you bring things down. We all help you. You understand me? Helen nods. I open the door to the building, and she follows.

You know we never had a lobby like this, I tell Helen as we wait for the elevator. But the minute one white person moved in management had the Super redo the entire entrance. Like ya can't see bare and ugly the way we can. We hop into the elevator.

And it's not that we don't like y'all—the hipsters, the doctors, the nurses, the people who gentrify. It's that we don't like that once we open the door to our community, everything changes. Everything. For your comfort. Not for ours. We've made comfort out of the conditions we've been served, and now ya just wanna run into what we created and change it without considering us. I feel the bitterness dwindle within me. It starts with the entrance, then ya want to control our customs, and next, none of our businesses are down the block. The elevator stops at my floor.

It wasn't my intention to make this community feel this way, but thank you for telling me, she says behind me.

☾

I sold and gave away every piece of furniture that had taken up space since before my birth. Helen moved out leaving her IKEA furniture to me.

Desmond's parents knock on the door, and none of us say a word. His mother walks in and examines business cards and key chains in a small bin I labeled *Desmond's Miscellaneous Things* with the tips of her nails. His father squeezes my shoulder and hands me a note before he squats down to lift the box labeled *Desmond's Belongings*. When they leave, I open the letter. His handwriting is still clear. He writes that he is better, claims that for a few weeks prior to the night on the bridge he had faked taking his meds, but now he is taking them regularly. It was the one condition his program mentor at the hospital gave after he had come clean about his disorder; the program couldn't afford a scandal especially one having to do with Black males and mental health. He found a place of his own, and he finally began talking to someone whom he paid to listen. *I apologize for becoming the enemy of your compassion. Love always and forever, Desmond.*

I sage every corner, every crevice of the only thing my mom left me: a rent-controlled apartment. I mix the last of the agua bendita with agua florida for a baño. I let the heat of the day dry my body. I oil all parts of me, between my toes, between my legs, behind my ears. I park my body on my couch. I turn on the fan, shut all the windows, close the curtains. I open the ice cream, serve the wine, and turn on Netflix.

There's a knock on the door. I inhale deeply and put on a robe.

El Super takes off his gray, beaten, work gloves and looks at me as he unzips his vest. Sorry to bother you, mi'ja, but I had a dream last night, and I have a message for you, he says. Your mom, esa mujer, she was so proud of you. She always said, Brother, me gané la loteria cuando tuve mi hija. I smile. She did claim I was her lottery prize on the days when the numbers she dreamed didn't match the ones announced. And I know, he says, she told me in the dream:

Tell mi Negra to be free.

So that's what you have to do, Eli, promise me, he says. Esa mujer era un show. She won't leave me alone if you don't listen. My eyes water, as I nod and then begin laughing hysterically. El Super joins in, slapping his gloves on his palms.

I have to help the new tenants, he says. Pero Morena, que you already know what I've told you since you were this high, he motions to his waist.

Chin up,
forehead up--towards the sky,
and ain't nowhere to go
except
pa'lante.

No hay ma' na'.

Habibi Beach Chair

On the intersection of Jerome and Gun Hill, in front of the Habibi bodega, Raul props open his beach chair. He slowly lowers his body, bending carefully at the knees, until he is sitting.

Although he knows he won't play, Raul shows up Monday through Friday with his left front pocket filled with a deck of cards, like he did back at the colmadón in La Vega. The sun fires up his deteriorating black 557 New Balances. He does not remember how he acquired them, but unless he thought intentionally about anything, he would not remember much before these shoes.

It wasn't that Raul didn't have the means to go back home—to sit at the colmadón and recreate the moments he once took for granted. It was that no one was left. The last time he asked his grandson to purchase his flight he packed his bags with razors, soap bars, and camisas to give out to his friends. The ones he never called, but he felt them resting in his hands like the calluses that had grown permanent from their days working in la loma together. When he arrived, he found most had died and the only one left was blind and deaf. He visited this man, had him feel his calluses, tried to see if it would ring a bell but there was nothing. After that, Raul told his wife he'd rather save el chin de dinero de el social security. Leave a little something for his children. The last time the Dominican Republic would see him would be in a casket.

The Bronx had become a home. And as many times as his descendants encouraged him to enjoy his last years on the island, Nueva York was the place that kept him alive. From this place he had gotten dialysis and bought some time. And now when he had nothing left of the community that he was forced to leave behind when his diabetes attacked his kidney, it gave him something else to get used to. From the beach chair, everything was a routine. The early morning filled with construction workers, school buses, and tired children. The early afternoon with addicts straddling a high, mothers running errands, and hospital workers looking for anything to satiate their hunger. The late afternoon held the freedom of teenagers, and the evening was simple with waste and grit.

Good morning, Habibi, Amr, the Yemeni store owner says. He squats besides Raul and pulls out a Marlboro. Raul returns the greeting always the same: by running his point finger over his throat in disapproval. Amr smirks lighting up his cigarette. Amr has always been curious about the life of this old man. He knows nothing other than he had taken to convert his storefront into his living room.

After a few quiet drags, Amr takes out his phone and flips to a picture of his wife. When he received it in an e-mail from his sister, his chest contracted.

Mira, Amr says. It's one of the only words he has memorized in Spanish. When he had come to the states, he swore it was English he'd have to learn. It was only after opening up the shop that he quickly learned it was Spanish he'd have to get comfortable with. He gives his phone to Raul and points at his ring.

Que bonita, Raul says kissing the cluster of the tips of his fingers. ¿Y donde 'ta? He twirls his wrist, his pointer finger at an angle, his hand becomes a question.

Yemen, Amr says as he points to the sky.

Traítela pa'ca, Raul says. He motions his hand from the sky to his heart.

Inshallah, Amr says. He brings his palms together to the center of his crown.

Si Dios quiere. Raul quickly bows his head. Si Dios quiere.

Pastelitos

They were starving. All he had in his fridge was a pack of la masa y un chin de queso. It wasn't the first of the month; therefore, he hadn't been able to borrow his mother's EBT card to make compras yet. There was rice under the sink and dried beans soaking on the stove.

She was new but already proved to be the smartest girl in Julia De Burgos High. Girls like her spent their time swimming in numbers and pressing up on books. But she was also a rebel and would curse a teacher out without using insults but by saying what she really thought.

Boys like him were not supposed to have girls like her sitting in their living rooms. She sat on his couch, the plastic still on it. She held onto her phone like it was a friend. He didn't know that her pupils were burning from the light on the screen, and she was trying everything not to look back at him. She had never cut school to be with a boy before.

He had never cut school at all.

You cook? She pouted her lips to point at the masa on his hands.

I know how to fry pastelitos.

Pastelitos ain't no real meal.

They good though, right? He didn't know how to cook rice and beans, but he knew how to fry something quick. He bent down to pick up the canola oil and ignored the small mouse scurrying around in the dark corners of the kitchen. From the oven, he bought out the frying pan.

Pastelitos de queso, he whispered to himself, his chest proud.

Con cachu?

Siempre, he replied. She shivered at the word always. Like he wasn't just talking about a food condiment.

You cook? He asked.

No, she moved closer to where he was. She tucked her phone into her back pocket. He unwrapped the masa, and set it next to her, cut a piece of white cheese and placed it on one of the sides of the circle. He wet the fork with water. Watch me. He folded the circle in half and it cradled the piece of cheese. He then used the fork to make dents along the edges that sealed the masa. Every time he pressed down, the veins on his forearms popped and she wanted to bite into him.

Your turn, he said.

She took the lead. Perfect pastelitos on her first try.

You smart, you real smart, he smirked.

They could survive anywhere.

He twisted the cap on the stove, put the back of his hand to his hip. He thought about all of the things he could teach her to fry. Why don't you know how to cook?

My dad wanted me to focus on school.

Ven, he said. He moved closer to the stove when the oil started crackling.

Throw it in there, you can do it, he said.

¿Tu 'ta loco?

The heat kicked louder and the oil yelled. And she prayed that the oil wouldn't get her face.

She slipped the uncooked pastelito into the pan and then they both hurried away, coming back only to turn the pastelito over.

When all four pastelitos were done they sat on the couch and dipped them into ketchup before biting into them. She covered her mouth and blew through her teeth.

Then they watched TV. He laughed loudly at *The Office*. She smirked, not sure what the joke was.

You don't get it?

No. My ESL teacher told me that it would take me a while to get jokes and metaphors in English. I've only been here eight months.

He's just stupid, he said.

Stupidity isn't funny to me anyway. She smacked her lips.

That's cause you're smart.

She only got A's in school. He didn't.

So are you, she said. He read thick books and said words her tongue could not twist to pronounce.

He smiled, twitching at his cheek. He didn't believe it but he liked to think he could be talented or smart.

During lunch periods, she wouldn't give him the time of day. He was tall and lanky, and his facial hair had come too early making him look like a dork instead of a man. She hung out with her girls, and her girls hung out with the basketball team. And he was not the type to jump or run. He liked to ride horses and teach them to dance bachata with his uncles back in Santiago. But then Mr. Rubin placed them in the same math working group, and their third partner got sick with the flu. That's when they got to talk while the rest of the class caught up with how quick they did their work. That's when she told him she wanted to cut school and he said, I got open crib, like he had heard other boys say. She smiled—all the confirmation he needed.

They played Uno, and when she won, she got up and hollered. !Es que yo si sé de esto! And he licked his lips. She bent at her waist and kissed him holding the back of his head. His mouth was warm, and her tongue felt like a flying thing to him. When she pulled away to breathe, the shame of being all the boys his mother told him not to be settled in his chest.

We don't have to, Mari.

I want to, she held his hand. I was the one that kissed you, Ulisses. No seas palomo.

His hands found hers behind her back. His fingers became a series of magnets that stuck to her. The lingering scent of cheese on her lips. She bit him softly and before he let go, to look at this girl who had just come from the island and was all brains, he tasted his own blood.

Yellow

The moon smirks down at me on Malcolm X Boulevard and Utica Avenue. It's Friday so most of our people are in the streets because being home is too personal to deal with. I go to a charter school two trains away. My family says I'm lucky. I got a real chance. There's no cops or liquor stores around campus. Around my place there's about eight spots in a single block radius. Cops come by every two seconds. There's dollar pizza cause we can't afford Italian. I cross through whole worlds each and every day. Under any other circumstance, I'd be a magician. But I'm Black, young, and hardly gifted.

YO! Samuel stops in front of a billboard.

My bro, Samuel, stops my thoughts like he always do. My moms say he bad influence. That he be hanging around me too much cause he got nothing else to do. But the shit he says stay taking me places I don't be willing to go alone. My science teacher, Mr. Freedman, says he's a catalyst. I think I believe him. He's from Santo Domingo, I Googled the translation, but truth be told, he ain't saintly at all. Stay calling his moms a ho and slapping his sisters after his dad found a new bitch to lay with.

How they don't have Curry on the cover? My mans is a LEGEND, he says. He stands on his tiptoes, hands in the air. Samy is thirteen and obese. He plays no ball, but he is great at keeping scores in the middle of folded napkins.

Today our history teacher said people who enter America, at entrance or at birth, were given boot straps; everything else, he said, is survival of the fittest. I know that's code for y'all ancestors was lazy. But really how we gon recover when all we got is NBA 2k17? I don't stay after class to ask. The textbooks are like The Bible and shit in these parts. I don't see the doctor or lawyer adults keep saying I could become. My sister tells me they're working through higher education at the moment. Yeah aight, they're just caught up in the books and the moves and left us for dead. She hit me when I said this. She's on a Fulbright at Columbia, but she still crossing worlds like me. Her school still made her take out loans to cover living expenses. Education is for suckers. I'm convinced.

I've asked my sister about advertisements in the hood. She says to look at the positive ones, so I try. There are other ads about leaning on your father for healthcare. What if you don't get along with the nigga? Do you still have a right to asthma pumps when your chest gets tight?

My big brother died from AIDS two weeks
ago, and no one except us, speak his real name.
My moms is stressed out. It costs my uncle a whole
lotta money to put my brother in the ground. My
moms promised to pay half of it back. This shit is all
a business—coming in and out takes major racks.
Yesterday, my moms was seconds away from
punching our landlord in the face, but my sister
rescued us. The landlord is Asian, and she don't
speak English when there's excuses. She do speak
just like them white folks when the rent is due
though. My moms hates that. She yells at me and
tells me to hurry on to school before I become a
good for nothing like my father. She don't mean it,
but it burns a hole in my chest for the rest of the
day.
　　　My first period teacher tells me to step out
when I laugh too loud. I could tell him, but
momma warned us not to tell a soul in school. Samy
don't even know, and I take the train with him two
times a day. If it slips, they'll take me away or
some bullshit. I wish I could ask some people up
there: How will that make anything better? Na,
better yet: how do you know that will make
anything better? I'd probably go out of my way to
look for AIDS or a fight then. If I'm not with my
momma, I rather be dead. Plus, my teacher
wouldn't care. He'll still say I'm obnoxious. They
think niggas like us can't breathe life into the dead
or laugh the turbulence away. I gotta go straight
home after school anyway. At the funeral, I cursed
out the lady who gave my brother AIDS. My sister
said she'd give me $23 dollars to apologize today.

The bitch works in Wall Street and she might be guilt tripped into giving us something. I doubt she gives a shit, she's probably just grateful her cells were stronger than my brothers and that she had the money to pay for the medicine that could've saved him. My sister says I don't get anything about life.

On the day of the funeral, it was sunny outside. Life is funny that way. It takes people from you and then it sends you a beautiful day. The whole day be fat with rays just giggling and wiggling at you a little bit when ain't shit funny. You don't need to frown, it says, at least you're the one living to see another day. My sister says forget our big brother cause he chose pleasure over breath, but I knew him.

He liked old ass jazz songs, and he made bead art when he was up late, thinking too much. He ate cornflakes because he said it kept him swole on the days momma didn't have enough to provide protein. Apparently, protein makes the muscle. My brother used to say white people went out of their way to make sure there wasn't enough of it in us. That muscle on us was only necessary 150 years ago when we picked cotton or shredded through sugar cane. If we ain't entertaining on the court or the field, they don't need us to be buff no more. They don't want us to go around getting the wrong idea, juno? My brother talked in lessons and stars like that.

I tried to tell my seventh grade teacher I knew poetry through my brother one time. She said his lessons weren't poems. They didn't lend themselves to moving forward or something. That was around the time I stopped raising my hand even when that make-believe light bulb went off. My brother kept reading his book when I told him. When the medication started getting to him, he lost all the weight. He bought a bunch of powder, but he threw it up anyway. They keep talking about balanced meals in homeroom.

They think a bite sized ham sandwich and some salad is enough for the hunger I carry. I have hunger to leap bridges and boroughs. How am I supposed to come up with the energy to grow and jump if momma be praying we sleep when she gets home just cause the spam ran out? They tell me to stop being greedy when I reach for another styrofoam plate at school. I've already had my turn or so they say. The extras go to the teachers to recover after a long day. But they get checks. The only thing I have is $23 dollars I haven't earned. I haven't even thought on what to spend it on. I would like a three-course meal to last me a few days, but my metabolism is crazy fast. I'm not ready to shit out $23 dollars just like that. My friend James brings food from home. His dad works for OVO, and he don't need the school lunch. The only reason he's even at this school is for the "diversity." He makes the line for me and passes it under the table. I be starving and no one listens because laws are written on rocks apparently.

Man let's go and try to get that tablet at the chicken spot! Samy says. I told you this nigga stay interrupting my thoughts. Always on some shit. I nod.

I'm down. I mean there ain't nothing else to do, I say.

The chicken spot machine is filled with lights and iPads. Samy been dying to get one. No matter how much he takes from his mom's bag it's never enough to afford one. Plus, he ends up spending his crumpled dollars on chips and 50 cent nutties after school. He spots me when he can. If I ever make it, he's the first person I'm hitting up. The line to the machine is dwindling. I love that word—dwindling. It rings for no reason. It just means you getting small; about to disappear at any second but the word sound like a burst.

It's my bro's turn. He misses right away. Samy's cheeks get a little red and I know he's a little upset. He got a bit of a temper, but he shakes it off. Let's get it, he says. He slips the dollar in, does a broken-up Harlem shake, and I cannot help but cover my mouth so he don't see me laugh. I hit the glass trying to get the tablet to shake. He's close this time but misses again.

Coñazoooo, he growls. I've heard that word so many times, and he told me it means power and anger. Whatever that means. There's a cop behind him getting some chicken. Samy got two more dollars, so I know it's another go. He focuses, but still he misses. He flips before I hold his shoulder the way I've learned to do when he gets upset.

He runs to the counter, I want my fucking money back! The Jamaican lady behind the counter shakes her head. I want my fucking four dollars back. He starts flipping chairs. The cop walks by him.

Chill, little man. I got you, he says.

Samy pushes a chair into him. I don't need your fucking money, you fucking pig! You traitor! You think you hot shit cause you Black with a badge? You ain't shit.

I start walking slowly towards Samy. His dad got arrested a couple of times, and I think it's cause of that he just don't like cops. But before I get to him the rattling sounds of handcuffs stiffens my body. I try to raise my hand now because I can't carry the silence. My moms tells me to stay away from the cops even when it's an emergency. You ain't handcuffing me! I'm 13, dumb ass nigga! Samy yells.

The cops puts them away. Listen, little mans, I don't want to hurt you. Relax. Take a break, the cop says. I'm going to get you and your friend here a meal.

Samy is completely flushed now. His eyebrows so tightly jammed together that they create the image of a crooked bridge.

We don't need you to feel bad for us, Samy screams. You dumb as fuck! WE. DON'T. NEED. YOUR. MONEY! Samy spits on the officer's shoe, and now there are four policemen inside the spot. One of them is holding a white bag. In a second, my brother is on the ground. He's in a straight jacket. His hands are being stuffed into sleeves.

The state can't afford to buy us coats for the cold, but they got the funds to wrap us up. I wish I would unfreeze to defend Samy, but my feet are cemented to the ground in bricks. I fight to raise my hand, but no one calls on me. I swallow the vomit that crawls up my throat.

Call my moms, Quante! Call my moms! I'm not fucking crazy. I'm not!

How we suppose to beat this if we can't react? How we supposed to know who is on our side? What if it would've been me that would've snapped? My feet start coming to life. I look down and my white uptowns are yellowing. I guess I'm just terrified about the possibility that there won't be a way out for all of us. That the moon smirks down only at a few of us and not at all of us. Like maybe the night sky ain't as big to hold every single one of us, and that maybe we all get by during the day because of the sun and its fake ass jolly ways.

Fire Fuego

Walking on mush, pavement, and concrete have never been Estella's thing, but she follows Solgone anyway. They walk past the tin roofed houses, past the Coca-Cola sponsored colmado, past the gate and the wandering cattle, into the finca, as if her chicken legs maintain their shape from jogging. *Lazy skinny.* Her body has never mattered because it is only her intellect people expected her to exercise. Solgone is jealous. Jealous that her own limbs were formed by forced work. *In this life, the last, and even the next, I am supposed to do the work because I was cursed and blessed with this solid body.*

Can we talk about her now? Estella asks. As if she was asking Solgone about last night's dinner and not about the falling of the moon.

Pa' que? The words are rusty as Solgone says them. She swallows attempting to lubricate her vocal chords; in the last five days, she had only opened her lips to meet the emerald mouths of Presidentes. Estella continues trekking behind her.

Being on her own had become a necessity for her. Since they arrived in Bonao, solitude seemed like a luxury. After la comida de las doces, she left their family home, yearning isolation. In the last week, she had not been able to process a breath before the next person announced themselves walking swiftly up the driveway. Mamá Girasol's church friends and extended family members had been coming in through the front door like an army of ants for the last three days. They refused to leave until they asked Solgone a string of questions; how is your mother? Your stepfather? What has changed about Nueva York since the trains? Why didn't you come to visit Mamá Girasol two years ago when the whole family came? Do you miss your older sister? She shrugged, shook her head, and gave an mmmhmmm when the answer was yes. When Mamá Girasol shot a look at Solgone, she shifted her lips to feign interest as best as she could.

They never mentioned her name though. Mamá Girasol didn't speak her name either. As if pronouncing the vowels would force her into swallowing her own tongue. Instead, she talked about those who had passed, about the people they had left behind, about the family split due to the separation of crumbs, until there was nothing else to say. She moved on to comment on the people on the outer perimeter of their lives. Every evening before the moon released the sun, Mamá Girasol excused herself and her mahogany rosary into her bedroom. At that time of day only God could hold her secrets up to the flame, she claimed. Solgone wanted to ask her if she ever prayed for Luna. If she felt Luna's soul deserved redemption, or if she figured she'd been assigned to hell. But even her own tongue wouldn't curl to pronounce her name.

Estella fills the last pocket in her lungs, and as she exhales, her breath drapes over Solgone's left shoulder like a heavy cloak. Estella calculates her breath with patience—*as if I really gave a shit.* Growing alongside Solgone had forced Estella to learn how to keep both of their needs in mind. Since they were kids Estella would bury her nose in Solgone's hair and apologize even when it was not her own fault. Solgone hardly stopped to consider Estella, unless there was someone other than herself coming for her. *Bouncing back from selfishness isn't easy.* Solgone wasn't always that way. When she was a kid, she was considerate of everyone except herself. She thought about her babysitter's son and his comfort while he took up space in something he considered his home. She thought of Estella and the wall their family had built around her to protect her petiteness, her ongoing anemia, her innocence. Even though they were the same age, born on the very same day, she was bigger and to adults less needing of protection. Instead of her father taking her to the library to exchange books like they were scheduled to on his days off, she thought of the many possible reasons he took her on his runs and exposed her to a world she was too young to see. Consideration of others led to self-loathing that suffocated her. Becoming the center of her own universe was how she managed to survive.

She inhales again, and Solgone imagines Estella's thin nose coming together and forming a single nostril. She exhales for twice as long as she had inhaled. 14, 13, 12, 11, 10, 9, 8, 7, 6, 5, 4, 3, 2, 1. Solgone can feel Estella controlling her rage—she wants to yell at her for disappearing as soon as Luna died, for refusing to be of help to anyone, for not talking about it with a soul, for leaving the family for three years. And still, Solgone expects her to bite her tongue, to say no more. Yet the words form in Estella's throat and stretch out like sprouting vines from her lungs. I've always loved you more than you love me, she inhales deeply again.

Solgone picks up her pace, the end of her flip flops spitting damp soil at the back of her knees.

You know something I realized while you were gone? Estella asks holding an answer in her gut. Today, I love women deeply because I learned how to love that way with you.

Solgone continues to walk onto the finca convincing herself that something waits for her there—anything but this conversation. She wants to be alone, but Estella has attached herself to her like a newborn. Solgone recoils. The memory was one she hated to remember and one her mind refused to forget.

Remember the time Luna caught us here? The question grows out of Estella's mouth prickly, cactus-like.

On their grandfather's land, they discovered one another's bodies in between the hanging of thick leaves of plátano trees and shrubs of cacao. Between the vegetation, the shrubs, and the length of the palm trees, they thought they were invisible. She had first learned from their babysitter's son and then studied it from an Anime porn she confused for cartoons in her father's stash.

On The Day, they realized they were running towards an ocean of alien pleasure, the land beneath Solgone's hands was moist from the thick rain that had fallen two days prior. Earlier that day, Mamá Girasol had watched the gray of the sky outside the door, and said, May hurricane season not be premature, so that you girls can get back home. Home was Nueva York where magic didn't exist at all. Solgone secretly prayed for the hurricane to come.

On The Day, they were surrounded and covered by green. They did what they were already comfortable doing. They lowered their shirts, exposing the painful lumps that had started to grow over their chest bones. Luna told them they were made by the moon to protect their hearts as they grew older and more vulnerable. They believed her. They worshipped these growing things. They kissed them and sucked them as the fire grew between their legs. But on this day, they graduated. They laid on each other—Solgone on top of Estella. The ball of fire grew, it grew as they moved.

And Solgone wondered if that's what happened to the boys and men who took without being given, the storm of the fire she felt at that moment. Was it the fuego that kept them from stopping when she said no?

Why do you have to do this right now? She turns to face Estella. Her face the same it has always been; fina, blanca, free from sin. There was not an ounce of change in her eyes or in the tone of her cheeks, but she was saying all the things she never said. Just shut the fuck up and go home if you can't walk in silence, Solgone says. Her voice at the same motion as a prayer. Her chest rises, and for that moment she feels taller than just five foot three inches.

Estella looks at her from where she stands and says, Do you think I'm queer because of you? She paces towards Solgone. Do you really believe that? The sun's rays slice Estella's face, and Solgone can only see one of her bright café colored iris turn towards the soil beneath them.

No. Solgone interlaces her fingers imagining them as perfect bows instead of weapons. The air sits like dead weight under her nose.

So why can't you talk about it then? We grown, Solgone. Estella folds her knees and sits on the ground, sucking her teeth, and shaking her head. Solgone paces around the space where she has fallen.

Because, she does not want to say it, but it's the only words that describe why she feels so disgusted. Incest. It's disgusting that it happened.

We were little ass girls, Solgone says and her skin feels like its covered in fleas.

Yet we already had needs and desires, Estella whispers.

OK, but it shouldn't have been towards one another. Again, what we did has a name—incest and probably fucking rape, man! Solgone yells. Estella laughs, her face towards the sky. And Solgone envies her for having no shame, for carrying no weight.

Luna found them On The Day, fixed their shirts, and patted the dirt off their backs. Did you like how it felt? she had asked. And when Estella said yes, she answered, You can do this with other people, when you want to, once you're older.

They didn't get in trouble, and no one else found out.

What are you laughing at? Solgone asks. You're torturing yourself for nothing, Estella says.

Nothing, she scoffs. She had heard Luna's words, but she had also seen her face fall.

We sucked each other's tits and dry humped, Solgone. There was zero penetration—we never even touched each other's pussies. Get over yourself, mujer.

Don't mention it! ¡Coño! Solgone covers her eyes with the palms of her hand. ¡Que asquerosidad, Dios!

Why the fuck not? It happened. Aren't you a truth teller? Is that not what you do? Speak your truth then. You can either learn to accept it for the natural aspect of it or continue to brood in self-hate.

You're downplaying it.

Ok, so tell me your perspective—your side or what not.

Solgone sits on the ground. Fruit flies and mosquitoes fly past her towards a piece of mango skin.

It wasn't just this innocent thing. We knew what we were doing was wrong. And before The Day, I led you to that bathroom every time. You followed me, and I hate me for being a fucking pervert, and I hate you for following me. Why the fuck couldn't we figure it out some other way?

Estella looks deeply into her eyes. We could've been raped, or we could've been touched by strangers, but at least we were safe. A toad croaks in the distance. She wants to tell her about their babysitter's son. About their older, distant cousins and the way, they adultified her body for their pleasure, but it's been so many years and those parts of her, who have lived with those stories, are tired.

I used to ask you to nibble my nipples and you were scared of hurting me, but you did it to please me. That's love. During that time, we were learning, and we believed that was the only real way of showing love towards one another. We were re-enacting characters in novelas and the shadows of our parents in the dark, she says.

According to Mamá Girasol, all of their grandfather's kin inherited the heat from him. Back in the day, despite how deep she was in religion, it was her favorite thing to yell at Marisol and María when she couldn't win. It came out her wide mouth like a testimony. Like it was one of the

things she believed in and preached in the
callejones. You all are the same. Igualitas a su
papá. Todos cueros. All pure hoes. María,
Solgone's mother, had decided to be brave one day,
Let's be honest, she crossed her arms on the table,
Word on the street is we just like you. Mamá
Girasol didn't take her next breath without
delivering a five-fingered imprint on her left cheek.
Pa que me respeten, she said as she walked out.

I had my first orgasm with you, Solgone
says. And once it is out there, she does not know
what to do or how to take it back. The single
orgasm has replayed in her mind for two and a half
decades.

The first time I came.
The first time I remember cumming.
The first cum I ever made.
The first time it happened.
I was 6 or 7.
I don't know exactly, all I remember is the feeling but
not my age.
It was an explosion between my growing hips.

We had our first orgasm together, Estella
ruptured the silence

Doesn't that make you uncomfortable?
No, because at that moment we wanted it.
And again, that's how we loved back then.

How do I love you now? Solgone asks.
Curious because she doesn't know if love is
something she does anymore. Estella shakes her
head in disbelief. You must know that I feel your
love. It's not the same way it must feel to be loved
by me, but it is still love, Sol.

111

How?

You called me. You're here today. After three years of not communicating with anyone, you chose me and we are here together. That is how our love works right now.

Thank you, Solgone whispers, I—I do love you, Estella, she cries. The phrase hasn't been formed by her tongue in years, and she is exhausted after she says it. Estella gets on all fours and moves towards her cousin. Once at her side, she holds all of Solgone's weight in her arms.

It feels like everything, yo, like everything, Solgone's voice cracks, that has happened as we've grown—the fuck-ups, the boundaries, have been because of that one thing, she blubbers into her chest. None of that is on you, Estella says. None of it. All that other shit is bigger than us. They sit in silence until the baby blue of the sky welcomes in orange.

When they stand up to walk back home, the crickets have begun their song and the fireflies dance as exposing their light power. Their Grandfather, Angel, used to tell them stories of fireflies; they weren't just insects. They held onto ancestors who still wanted to watch over their descendants on the physical realm.

Seriously though, Estella says.

What?

Can we talk about her now? Presidentes on me, she smiles.

Ahhhhh come on. Solgone opens the gate to exit the finca. Fine, I can commit to that con una fría.

Walking has never been Estella's thing, but she walks behind Solgone, protecting her back against the darkness.

Romo

If the rum had not spilled, you would not have figured out the stretch of your strength.

But the rum did spill like a tiny lake. In one breath, the amber liquid conquered a single white tile on the kitchen floor. The glass shattered at the rim and you swore under your breath a thousand times.

Coño, coño, coño, coño.

You had not meant for your fingers to soften their grip on the perspiring glass.

You had fought for that ice. Trained yourself to keep the refrigerator closed for the length of a full day to ensure the water would condense. After a long day of work, of teaching English to adults with dreams you knew transcended reality in New York, you just wanted to have a hard cubicle of water swimming and cooling down your favorite mixture of Brugal añejo, a splash of passion fruit juice, and a squeeze of lime.

After you examined the amber, you glance towards the shadow of the light fixture on the old living room couch. The electricity was out again but one could still count on the moonlight for the essential sights.

The apartment you inhabited was small. Even for the standards of someone who had never built a dream of departing the island. But it was all you could afford. Even here. Even paying in pesos. The space was so constraining that the heat had nowhere to go and it just ate at your limbs along with the insects.

From this window, I like to think you did mean it.

The rupture.

The shatter.

On another dusk, you would have gotten on hands and knees. Licked and slurped the rum off of the tile floors. Glass and all. No doubt.

Yet, the amber liquid landed on the ceramic tile like a small lake and you could not remember the last time you had plunged all 163 pounds of you into a body of water. Even after picking up and moving here—your grandmother's barrio, the one she told you never to return to—you had never taken a trip to la playa.

You packed the bathing suit like going to the beach at this time of night was normal on an island like this one. You left the rum bottle behind. Did not bother to clean the lake off of the floor.

You hailed a motoconcho, who to this day is heard saying he advised you against the trip. He dropped you off at a small beach by Boca Chica.

The Caribbean presents itself as calm even at dusk.

I like to think you walked into the depth of the ocean and enjoyed the way it altered your breath. I like to think you saw something better than this.

On the ninth day of your disappearance, after a work friend reported you were missing to the police, I went into your apartment.

The rum bottle was on the countertop. The tiny lake had dried into a brown stain. I walked into your room to see your luggage still packed and the closet still empty.

You were never here to stay.

Heaven

Mad people is up here populating heaven, or whatever this is place is, it's like there ain't a limit. I walk for a long time, opposite the direction of the crowds and I find her sitting on the grass. She digs her tiny fingers into the soil and pulls out the blades from the roots. Each time the grass comes back longer and longer. Her face is blank, not as amazed at this stuff as I first was when I arrived here. Princess in pink rhinestones is spelled out against the front of her headband.

Hey, I say sitting next to her. The size of her purple tutu skirt doesn't make it easy to tell where the fabric ends and her body begins. Her feet move side to side in her white shoes. What's your name?

Sade, she responds.

I'm Jay R, nice to meet you. I hold out my hand to notice that her hand is small but her grip is mighty.

What is this place? She looks around. The movement gives me a chance to get a good look at her head. It's bald and shiny, at the top there is a deep scar.

Well—

Is this where Papa Dios lives?

I explain that I don't know if this is the place. That I am not sure there is a Dios. Her eyes water, and I see heartbreak in her chest. Is there anyone?

Just people who have passed on earth, I cough. What happened to you?

I had cancer. She points at her head. I nod trying to look as surprised as I can. I'm dumb for having even asked. She looks like one of those St. Jude's kids after all.

You?

I was killed by mistake, I respond. I don't know why I answer the question anymore. Every time someone arrives, we receive divine information on how they got here, but it seems it's normal for everyone to ask anyway.

She giggles, No one dies by mistake, Jay R. Wisdom sits on her eyes and I feel like I can't make sense of anything for a minute. I take a deep breath. The people who came for me planned it out perfectly, I start. They just had the wrong guy. It wasn't me. It was all just a big, complicated mistake.

☾

My death was so slow that opening my eyes to this wasn't a surprise or a scare or nothing. If I had survived, I'd be the hood's Jon Snow or something; I mean that sort of thing would've been impossible. Death just was what it was. I mean I had feelings about it, for sure, but I knew off the bat, when I opened my eyes after the white screen, my life as Jay R was over. There was nothing I could do.

On earth, when I first started to think through death, I did not have a single version of the afterlife. I had an asopao type understanding of la muerte—a little bit of everything.

The first version came from my sister. My sister was lyrical cause she always had her music app on and her headphones in. If her voice was not so low, so squeaky, so gentle, she could put Cardi B to rest. But she loved Cardi B so much she wouldn't even if she could. She told me death was like the track she played over and over when our cousin, Nana, was beat to death by her boyfriend in Santiago, "I'll be Missing You."

So basically, death is like wanting someone to be back but not ever seeing them again? I asked.

No, Jay R, dang, that's not it, she rolled her eyes. Why you always so literal about everything? I shook my head. Why you always so literal about literally everything?

Ok, I said, tell me how then.
It's like, "Yo Te Extrañaré," the song they played at her funeral. Ok? It's like having an angel watching for life.

I got another story from Mami who said in death Justice was finally made by the hands of God. If you'd been a shit head on Earth, you'd go to hell. But if you were ok. A white lie here. A little lie there. A few bucks from a purse without permission, and you still had it in you to pray. Like fine, God would give you a second break after putting you in purgatory. And if you were a straight saint, like my Abuela, you'd go straight to the good place, no questions asked.

Then there was my favorite story. The one I learned in ninth grade Social Studies. Coming back again. I'd imagine I'd come back as a president. Fix all this shit up. The minute I found out, I told my sister. She sucked her teeth so hard Mami came in.

¿Y que pasó? Mami wanted to know. Jay R believing everything these blanquitos say. My sister took everything that came from a white person with a grain of salt.

It's not them, I tried to explain, It's an eastern belief. Like people all over Asia think that's what happens. I'm just telling you so you don't waste time missing me because imma be gone living my next life. Mami pushed my head playfully and curled a strand of my hair around her finger. I loved when she did that. It calmed me down. Her touch reminded me that she loved me, that I was half of her heart.

My life is, I mean was, fine. My mom had a job, my dad paid child support and he came through sometimes, took me to baseball games. Sometimes I'd like a girl too much and that shit would have me listening to Drake, but you know what? It was ok. I had my first kiss just seven months ago. When I pulled away, she said I was a good kisser, and even though I wasn't crazy about her badly dyed orange blonde hair, I thought you know what? I could do this. My grades were mostly B's and C's, I was on the baseball team in the spring. My teachers loved me because I used a lot of my free time to help out after school. During the summer, my mother would give my sister and I the option to go to Florida with my uncle's family or to the Dominican Republic with my grandmother. We always chose DR.

Even though I was fine, the world wasn't. It still isn't. In the life that was taken from me, I was preparing to be a cop. My friends didn't like that, but I wanted to fix both sides—the crooked cops and the straight up delinquents. In another life though, I would come back as a president. Fix some shit like I said. Put some computers in public schools, so kids didn't have to wait two months to touch a computer to type an essay. We could learn more like that. I would put money into the hoods. I would open up after school programs with programs kids actually like. The house would call me a thief and I would laugh. On the paper it would have said: President Fernandez is changing the United States. You know, it ain't that hard. I don't know why they be bugging, acting like the little shit they do is all there is to give. Give these little boys and girls something to do. Maybe that way they wouldn't have killed me. Give these people a better way to cope. Maybe if they had something to pass the time with, they would turn to violence.

I'm getting distracted. Talking about a life I'll never have again, you heard? That's it. It's gone. Done. That's what everyone up here keeps telling me. I met so many other boys killed the same week as me. I met some girls too. I've seen some famous people. They just normal up here, so I told BIG about that song my sister loves, and he said, She will, you know? She'll be missing you until the very end. And then I felt it, the tear. You cry up here, too.

That's another thing: we're a ball of feelings. The soul. Here and there. Emotions run high too. It's just up here we are guided by something outside of our feelings. I don't know what it is yet. It's just up here everyone is listening to one another, getting on all the things because they trying to figure out what it looks like next. Earth. Life. Existence. After humans. After the bodies rot.

I wish I had more time. I blame the guys that did this. That mistook me for a crook I wasn't. I blame them. Of course, it's on them. They did the thing. They were the ones that dug the machetes into me like I was nothing but a sheep, a pig.

☾

Since I've been here, I haven't spoken to many folks. I was the talk of this place for what seemed forever, and I got tired of repeating and repeating and repeating that I had been murdered. Up here—there is no home. Everything is open space. Everyone and everything is out and about, communicating even when they don't necessarily want to. On Earth, it seems solitude was important, but here everyone, regardless of differences flows together. We are balls of energy and together we are a force. I don't know how I know any of this, but I do.

Most days I stand next to my mom and watch the heartache contract her chest like a faja squeezes in fat. I have to reach into her body to remind her everything is fine. Up here, her soul understands, and it sends a wave that relaxes her. I'm grateful for whatever started us because they started with the soul. Imagine it hadn't? People would just be dying of heartache left and right and right and left. I have to watch out for my sister. She used to watch out for me. She talks to me sometimes. I listen and respond but she can't hear me. She feels me though, and I think that's keeping her afloat. But today I decided to leave her and my sister alone. Here it's all different and I haven't really gotten to see none of it at all. Ever since I died, I can't take a moment to take in fully where I am. My entire block cries for me, people who do not even know who I am pray for me, there is so much anger and agony in the streets I once walked. How can I rest?

☾

This morning there was a shift and I was just glad it did not involve me. When I found her on the grass, I just wanted to talk a little bit and not argue. But she keeps looking at me like I'm lost and she's right.

You didn't die by mistake, she says jumping to her feet. As she hovers over me, the ball of emotion bangs inside of me.

I did, I yell. I'm a fucking jerk for yelling at an eight-year-old, but I do. All she has for me is a smile—a glowing pumps out her, first from her head and then from her feet.

It was time, she says. Your mom and dad are going to love each other again in your absence, something their pride would've never allowed them to do if life on earth had not been disrupted. Your sister will learn the lessons she was sent to learn a lot quicker. And you, she whispers with a smirk, you avoided a life you really wouldn't have wanted.

You can't just say that, little girl. That's not enough of a reason for me to die! I stand up, balling my fists, and squaring up. And I have to stop from laughing at myself because I'm sure if I laugh, I'll also cry.

On the other hand, she laughs hysterically patting her small belly and taking a few steps towards me. She extends her hand and runs her tiny fingers over my knuckles. You can't be angry forever, Jay R, this isn't earth.

I know, I growl. The ball of emotion within me slows down again. I'm not exactly mad, I say. She tightens her grip around my hand, and the tears start coming again. I just had so much to do, I say. The tears come, and I open my arms, lift my head, and sob taking in the vastness around us.

Tu 'ta loco? You've done so much already. People have come together from everywhere.

Gangs are uniting. Guess who could never do that? She doesn't wait for my response and laughs, THE POLICE! It's like an inside joke for her and the laughter brings tears of joy to her yes. I wipe my face and laugh with her.

You know what I've done? She asks. I raise my eyebrow in a question.

I helped the people around me understand that love isn't about holding onto someone forever, it's about being grateful and letting go.

Her limbs begin to expand and grow. She becomes a teenager, an adult, an old person right before my eyes in what feels like a single second. The smile on her face quivers but doesn't change.

The transformation ends in a bag of brown skin and bones that stretch it into some sort of shape. The clothes she wore fall to shreds into the space around her as gentle as petals.

The love we make, she whispers, as family, friends, and lovers it's like a street taking us to somewhere poquito a poquito until—

She explodes into stardust.

Everyone around me rejoices. I wonder when they made their way towards us. They hug each other like they've regained life itself or clap as if we've just landed in the Dominican Republic.

Let it be my time! I hear man shout. I don't understand the joy in the explosion, but my soul glows and I know Justice was made.

Mi'ja

Hola Toni, y mi primita Yally, is she here? No, no one is home. *Ok, if I go get Nati, can we play in the kitchen?* Let me show you something first; *Is that a worm?* Something like it. Sit on my lap. *Mami says I can't sit on anyone's lap.* How old are you now? *4 and a half;* Wow, you're a big girl. Take off your shirt. *No.* Don't tell me no. Let me see; do you like that? Stay. Don't go. *It does not feel like anything.* Take off your underwear. *No.* Don't tell me no, tu quieres una pela? I'm your family. You have to do what I say. *Eso me duele. Stop. Please. I want my daddy.*

Go home. Don't tell anyone, or I'll kill your Daddy. *El te mata a ti.* Cállate, Malcriada. Además, he has no papers, he can't come back here. *I'll tell Mami.* This also happened to her. No one will believe you. *Why?*

131

☾

2009

I like things when they hurt. That's what
Mami says like she knows me better than I know
myself. She says I wouldn't know happiness if it
reached for me, if it touched me, if it held me. She
says that I have always had una cara de terrorista.
That I came out of her already upset like I had to
fight off the devil himself inside her womb. She
loves to remind me that the doctors had to spank
me repeatedly to get me to pretend to cry. I roll my
eyes at this story every time, but she asks que
¿quien yo me creo? She asks why am I so hell bent
on becoming someone no one has a taste for. Mami
only says this when she realizes she doesn't
understand me. When the frustration of not
knowing her own daughter makes her detest
herself.

I am seventeen, but I feel like a trillion.
Mostly because I don't die. I always come back up
for more life. In grandmothers, and daughters, and
daughter's daughters. In everybody I keep
making the same mistake. I do not know what
mistake that is entirely, but I try not to repeat it
again. Either way, I appear here. Reoccurring. All
over. Alive again.

Papi says que yo soy la negra mas bella de
el planeta tierra. He says it with so much gusto in
his tongue that I almost feel like I am a worthy
thing that should not listen to my mother.

Your mother is just fearful, he says. She
never let anyone love her. Not until she met me,

and that took me long time, mi'ja. Long, long
years, but we made you.

Papi is the only good man alive I am
convinced. He is committed to the cause of not
hurting Mami or me. He says he's known too
many men who drown in power only to come up
empty and indebted to women who try everything
to free them. His own father was nothing like him.
He worked for Balaguer and assassinated people in
the name of La Patria. He came home and hit
Mamá Antonia. His own brothers are his enemies
because they took after their father and think Papi
is a pendejo.

I know I am a thing, not supposed to be tied
to a body, but relationships like the one I have with
Papi keep me anchored here. I want to go. Many
times, I flee. I am seventeen on this trip, but I am
really a trillion. I wish I did not know I was. I miss
the freedom that lies behind this existence. I miss
the freedom of wandering into realms and exiting
swiftly without making mistakes. My mistake this
time around I think is loving Pa. Or is it that I
remember what I should have erased when I was
tricked into remaining here?

☾

Tomorrow is my high school graduation.
Mami takes me to the salon and says yes to the
keratin treatment they say I need pa aflojar los
moños. Mami has nice hair. Hair that feels like the
top of rocks under the Masipedro River— smooth

and deliciously slimy. Mami's hair needs none of this gunk that burns my eyes under the secador. She holds the towel to my eyes, pressing her fingers into the back of my eyelids.

Tu si eres mojona, mi'ja, she says, how much can it burn? I want to kick her shins and see her bleed. But I bite my tongue, bite it until I taste the bitter blood that sends a release into the tips of my feet.

At the chair, the lady, who I call Tía because I have known her since she put my first relaxer in at four, keeps burning my scalp with the blow dryer and saying, Sorry, sorry, Mami. It doesn't hurt me too much, but I catch her in the mirror winking at my mother like they're in on something. Like their goal is to skin off my scalp, and I wish I could burn this whole place down.

Papi drives by the salon in the minivan he used to deliver goods and products to bodegas. He smiles when he sees me. When I climb into the back seat, he stares at me through the mirror, tu eres una estrella como quiera, he says.

Esa muchacha, all she does is complain, Mami says putting her seatbelt on. And Papi shakes his head. He never says anything. I wonder who taught him silence is better than yelling, and I wonder why I picked it up from him.

☾

Graduation day. I have three friends. I have chosen the three of them because they have made it easier to hide through high school. Jimena

is in the student council. She has thick, black hair
and when people call her Mexican she corrects
them and tells them she is indigenous. Layla is tall
and beautiful in the traditional way. Even one of
our teachers called her refined, and ever since she
lies about being Amelia Vega's cousin. Her
afternoons are packed at the nail salon across the
street doing feet and sweeping floors. Sahana has
skin like silk, and she takes off her hijab every time
she enters the school doors. She runs the coding
club, and we often take the train back home in the
late afternoon. She is the only one I have told about
being four.

My friends are gorgeous and brilliant, but
they don't carry hurt like me. They put it to sleep
every day, and only wake it up at night behind
closed doors. I wish I had that power. But I don't.
My hurt lives on my face and I struggle to mask it
up en vivo every day.

Sarai Magdalena Martinez, my principal
calls. Everyone cheers, teachers and students. I
have always given them what they want. From the
stage, I see Papi running down the aisles with his
camera. I shake my principal's hand, hug some of
my teachers, and walk down the stairs. Papi is at
the bottom. His hair stands like a fluffy cintillo
around his head. It's been receding but he refuses
to get rid of what is left. The texture is just like
mine. I almost hate him for passing it down. But I
smile for him. So big and so wide that I almost
believe joy can prosper inside of this body. I almost
believe that life will be smoother in college.

Squeezing into aisles is the worst for me because there is a lack of personal space. My body has decided to stretch into places I did not ask it to in the last two years.

¡Leona! I hear a small whisper. I turn as I am squeezing to my seat and see it's Emmanuel.

The first week of junior year, I let him kiss me in the back staircase after school. He put his fingers under my uniform skirt, and it felt ok, but I bit him accidentally, and he pulled back scared.

What the fuck are you— a vampire?! He said touching his lip.

Put down the fucking Twilight, you fag, I whispered. He looked pleasantly surprised, and I immediately wished I hadn't.

Maldita animal, fucking leona, he said. There was blood on his lip.

Here, I said. I went in my crossover bag and got a napkin. When he came in for it, I pulled him into me, cleaning off the blood with my tongue. It was sweeter than mine. We had sex for the rest of the year. Other than some pain, I didn't bleed the first time like all the books said I would.

Leona, he whispers again. I swing the back of my foot for his leg. But I don't hit him; instead, a nail digs itself into my Achilles tendon. The rush of delight spreads, and I have to bite my tongue to calibrate the pain. I move quickly towards my seat, trying not to slip on my own blood. Wiping the sweat off of my forehead I sit.

Papi is outside when I exit the school grounds, and Mami is as shy as a mouse standing behind him with flowers and a balloon, her face growing out of his shoulder. I am so proud of you, he says. He kisses my forehead and tightly squeezes my shoulders.

Mi'ja, Mami whispers, for you. Fifty red roses. I have never gotten flowers before, but I know these are expensive. Her eyes are watery and she reaches out for the four chords around my neck. A daughter with honors, she opens her arms to me. I am honored to be your mother. I let her hold me. I squint my eyes trying to will myself to feel for her what I feel for Papi. But it won't sprout.

Mr. and Mrs. Martinez, my assistant principal approaches us, looking at the floor. She raises her eyes to look at me and then she crouches to look at the back of my foot.

Are you ok, Sarai? Papi lifts my gown.

Ahy dios mio, Sarai, mi'ja, Mami bends to see. It's a hole, Samuel, she says. Let's go, let's go to the hospital. Papi takes the roses from me.

I'm ok, I protest. Part of me is angry that I'm being touched and examined when there is nothing wrong. The other part of me is alleviated.

There's darkness.

☾

2010

I will cut your tongues and make salsa rosa si me le dicen loca una vez más a la muchacha, Mami yells. My tias' cheeks grow red and I know they won't ever call me crazy for going to therapy again. Mi'ja, Mami whispers.

The smooch she plants on my cheek breaks the silence. Papi smirks. The first sign of joy I have seen since I told them everything.

☾

2012

Hey. How was your week?
I think I'm dating someone.

Tell me about them.
They are nice. They always try to do things to make me smile when I see them in the Latinos Unidos group. But on Monday they asked me out for coffee, and I said yes. We went to Moonie's last night. They tried to kiss me but I stopped them.

Did you want them to kiss you?
Yes, but I am scared.

Scared of what?
Myself.

What do you think you'll do if they kiss you?
I'll like it.

What if you like it?
I'll hurt them.

Because someone hurt you?
I guess.

Do you think you still like things when they hurt?
I don't know.

What brings you happiness now?
I guess
                    existing here
                                        and now.

I am a trillion, but I am still learning.

The Law

One, two, three heartbreaks at the hands of
men no longer do it for women in your generation.
You do not seem to learn lessons until they
cause aches.

☾

New Year's Eve 2015. I wore a strappy,
black dress and thigh high black boots. My afro
would have reached the heavens if I would have
willed it to. One of Talia and Dalia's cousins from
their father's side was the first to see me walk into
the room. I had masked myself in confidence.
Back in the day, I was attracted to him. Attracted
to the fact that he was an older man that bought me
the things my teenage heart desired. He was fifteen
years my senior and had a goatee that drove me
crazy. Once I even let him pick me up from my
part-time job. He flirted with me in a parking lot,

and I giggled at the things he said even if I was just uncomfortable. When I didn't laugh, he said I was young, and I believed my discomfort to be a sign of my immaturity. On our way home, he stopped at the park, kissed me, licked my neck, and pulled down my shirt bringing my bra down too. He opened his mouth to my breasts and then said he imagined I had areolas the size of dollar coins and because they were larger it showed that I was a full-grown woman. Now he stared at me with his daughter bouncing at his hip and his wife at the table behind him with their son, as if I were the last Coca-Cola on Earth. My stomach turned. I walked away giving him a smile— only de cortesía.

I had lost a significant amount of weight over the summer. Throughout the night, everyone told me so. Te vez divina. Divine. The few times I stepped into the bathroom I touched the flatness of my stomach and felt empty. The end of this year had been rough. Ronnie had called it quits despite the ways I over extended and eventually completely erased my boundaries for him. We were weeks away from moving in together. I had already bought a lamp and a mini bar for the living room. One day, he just texted that he had to end it. He claimed he wasn't yet content with himself. That he had little to offer me. That he could no longer commit to a relationship until he was a well-rounded man. I believed him until my sister, Kiara, saw him out with someone else. I know men lie. I'm not dumb. I know men will run circles around our heads, but his life was so extraordinarily close to mine that I hated him for flushing three years down the drain like nothing.

The betrayal was so debilitating I didn't even bother getting up for work. After my seventh day of no call, no show, I lost the highest paying job as a communications director at a health non-profit. Fortunately, I had saved a little something, and I got picked up by another non-profit three weeks later. My friends tried to do their best, but I drove them away. The last time I had spoken to Leila she suggested that if I was just lonely, I should jump on Bumble or Tinder or something. You need dick, she promised, that is it. Trust me.

But it was New Year's Eve and so I danced with Papi, and I let Mami introduce me to a million more of her friend's children. This year Mami and Papi got everyone to put in a little something for this rental hall. The DJ they hired installed multi-color disco lights that moved in waves and el pueblo bought half a dozen kids that ran after them.

My parents were once the couple that threw el party por la ventana in the 80's and 90's. Parties full of sweat and loud bass. Kinito Mendez and Sergio Vargas even dropped into them at some point. Ahora people just wanted a decent sized danced floor, an array of dishes--moro de guandules, un pescado, una carne, un pastelón, una ensalada, una pasta, and somewhere to bring their grandkids. That was the other thing.

Everyone was having kids. Even Kiara had little Papito, and his perfection made my ovaries twitch. Even though my parents weren't thrilled about her baby daddy, they love the baby like they did not have a purpose before him.

The minute Mami let go of me I joined Kiara, Talia, and Dalia by the DJ booth. We updated one another on the latest chisme in our lives, and I laughed at the way we are still just kids in these bodies. Dalia went away to Ghana to volunteer with her school and she told us about the joy in folks and how they asked questions about where she was from but didn't ask the white kids. Papito pulled Kiara to the dance floor, and they danced to a merengue on one single spot. She picked him up and moved her hips to the merengue, her face pressed against his, like she wasn't upset baby daddy chose to be with his boys tonight. Someone else to consume your thoughts and energy, I thought maybe that was the heaviest pro on going half on a baby.

At 11:43 p.m. I stepped out into the twenty-three-degree weather because I needed a cigarette above all else. Before I took out the box of Newport 100's, I fast walked down three blocks and turned a corner just to make sure no one could see me. Taking the first drag of the cigarette I closed my eyes and admitted to myself that depression was visiting again. I snuggled into my oversized coat.

The piercing sound of the wind dancing through the city blocks silenced his arrival. As he turned the corner, he looked at me, and then he did a double take. Men did that a lot, so I shrugged—a simple acknowledgement. The thing with men is you can't ignore or deny them. And even when you let them know you see them, you still risk danger. He walked towards me, and inside my coat pocket I started to twist the fake diamond ring around my finger while preparing the I'm- engaged-line.

Before I could begin my role, he threw himself on me, grabbing my coat, the Newport fell, and I felt his nose aggressively pressed into my palm as I screamed and tried to push him off. The size of his limbs worked to his advantage, and he managed to jam his knee into my vulva, while slipping his fingers into the bottom of my coat and then my dress.

The music from near and distant house parties wrestled with a panicked inner voice, and I was sure I would not be heard.

☾

He came out of nowhere. You didn't ask for him. You weren't looking. In fact, you were avoiding. That is what you say forgetting you prayed to be saved.

Today you know, he jumped out of the car, pulled him off of you, and punched him in the jaw. Without taking a look at you, he called the police even after the perpetrator ran away. He asked you if you were ok as he vacillated between getting in his car and going after the guy or staying out with you. No, you cried loud and deep. A lie would've hurt you more than the man's calloused fingers and dry palms groping you like he owned you. The cops arrived forty minutes later only to ask for a brief description. Thank you, you said after they left.

Your makeup is smeared, he said offering tissues.

If you have nothing else to do, you're more than welcome, you said dabbing your tears.

When you re-entered the party with him, and your parents asked what took so long he extended a hand and said, She stepped out to get me. I'm Kevin, a friend. Your mother raised her left eyebrow. Your father translated. His eyes asked a question: are you ready, mi'ja?

He was tall, light skin, and had gaps between his teeth that made him look dorky and sensitive. His deltoids and tricep muscle bulged from under his gray sweater as he brought the glass of Johnny Walker (your father had poured for him) to his lips. Las mujeres asked questions, trying to communicate via facial expressions, but you felt a high going along with the lie. It was better than the truth.

Your father asked you to dance again. This time it was Anthony Santo's "Creíste". You always danced but this time you danced, danced knowing his eyes were on you. Danced thinking of how in a second everything could shift; grateful a shitty altercation turned into a gift. Danced holding onto the bachatero's words—Creíste que después de ti se acabaría la vida. You felt uplifted knowing that heartbreak was no one's cause of death.

He wanted you. Of course, he did. So, after la fiesta, after he dropped off all the relatives he could fit into his back seat, he asked you out for lunch.

☾

On January 1st, he took you across the bridge to a Cuban restaurant in New Jersey. In the car, he asked you questions that made you feel important. You turned up "Love Yourz" by J. Cole when the song came on. After the song was over, he said the song had reminded him to appreciate the generosity life had extended to him, a boy who grew up in Jersey with an alcoholic white dad and an Antiguan mother, who remained in an abusive relationship because he had purchased the family home that put a roof over relatives who came to the States. He took a deep breath, cupped his chin, and said he couldn't believe he had just told you that. You smiled and reciprocated by telling him that your dad too had dark days.

He asked you what he should order, and you encouraged him to get ropa vieja, the most Cuban item on the menu. You got sautéed shrimp and steamed vegetables. You both ate in silence having had shared too much already. You chewed as politely as you knew how to, swallowed, and drank water before asking, So what do you do?

He wiped his mouth before telling you he was a lawyer. Five years as a criminal justice attorney. He claimed he began his journey into law in the name of his boys who had been locked up

147

when he had not; his way of making sure he used his privilege to fuck this system. He was trying to start his own practice soon. And you said that was nice, interesting, but inside you were saying: This is him. Finally, ¡Gracias a Dios!

You asked about his most frustrating cases. He said it was anytime innocent men were falsely accused. I have sisters, I have a mom, I have friends who are females. I believe women, he said, but I also see the culprit in women as much as I do in men. I hate to see a Black man down. I hate to see one of us be kept away from our own children because things didn't go the way the women wanted them to.

Your sangria came, and you thanked the waiter, secretly grateful for the interruption and the alcohol. You sipped and asked, Well, do you think these women are telli—

I mean someti—

He caught himself and signaled with his hand for you to finish asking your question, you tightened your lips and shook your head.

Listen, Karla, right now all the buzz is sexual harassment due to the Me Too and Times Up movements. And I'm with it! My problem is that these feminist movements have made it, so men are automatically guilty without a fair trial. He placed his hand over his mouth and expanded his chest as he quietly belched. It's not right, he continued, I have seen the images of good men torn to shreds. I've seen them lose their careers, kids, homes, and entire support systems all before the court has labeled them innocent or guilty.

You nodded instead of naming what you were thinking—good defense didn't automatically mean truth or justice.

The conversation shifted to you. You said you worked for a non-profit that cared for homeless families. That you loved what you did, but you wrote stories, and you wanted to pursue that head on. He asked to see some of your work and you smiled. You asked him about his favorite fiction book, and he didn't have any except, *The Alchemist.* He read it in college and it changed my life, he claimed. You nodded.

He drove you home. And there was a discomfort you couldn't name. As you took off the seatbelt, you expressed gratitude for lunch and for the saving on New Year's Eve. Don't mention it, he said. You leaned into him surprising yourself and him. He pulled you off only to tell you were beautiful and that he was sorry you met the way you did but lucky, nonetheless, he could hold you now. As you kissed again, he touched your back, felt your legs, and led your hand to the pumping of him. Even though you continued to kiss him, you hardly moved your hand. I'm sorry, he said, It would be smart to wait for that, huh? You smiled, removed your hand, and bought your lips to his. The sun went down, and the windows became foggy and you both were still kissing and caressing each other in his car.

That was the most unforgettable New Year's Day I've ever had, he texted you. 2016 is off to a great start. Thank you.

☾

For six months, you met once, maybe twice a week. He was busy. You were busy. This was a grown ass, power couple relationship. He lived in a condo out in Jersey City, but he crossed the bridge to you. Rented a hotel or stood over at your place. Made you breakfast in bed. Left you notes in places you wouldn't find until later in the week when you had to control your urges to beg him to come to you or convince him to let you go to him. But he was busy with cases and people who needed to be defended and saved.

You found your way to your friends again and they told you this was it. You had to stop being paranoid.

Why do you always do this, Karla? You deserve this. You deserve a grown ass man, they cheered. You had to put a pause on your trauma. You couldn't let it ruin a good thing.

But you didn't listen. You Googled him, went on his social media pages, looked at all of the pictures he had liked, all the images that pushed him to leave comments. You didn't understand why he was so prone to like pictures of women when he had the entirety of you. The questions erupted out of you on the fourth month. Why haven't I met any of your family or friends? You've met many of my folks already. He assured you the time would come. You pressed on and on. He answered the line of questions you had by saying he understood that your past made it, so you didn't trust, but he had nothing to hide. He was yours. Your time would come, you'd see.

Puerto Rico was a gift he sprung out of nowhere. It proved his case, you were reacting out of what you had been through, he was a good man. A gentleman. Every morning he woke you up and he eased your stress with what was good between his legs. He let you order him around and teach him the things you liked. He told you he could get used to you. You believed him. When he went into the bathroom, he left his phone out, and you tried to get into it but there was a password. You're fucking crazy, you thought, you don't want to do this again. The devil was not going to win by putting doubt into your head.

Every night your knees met the ground below the both of you. You wanted the pleasure to help erase the contradictions in you. Babe, chill with the saliva, he moaned. In that moment, with your throat filled with him, he made a case the abundance of wetness didn't allow the friction between your lips and his skin to exist.

☾

Back in the tristate area, things went back to normal for a sometime. And then you didn't see him for two weeks and then three.

You called. You texted. He showed up for an hour after the sixth week. He claimed he was busy being a lawyer, a son, a brother, a boyfriend to you. He was tired. And so, you had him lay down and massaged him with oil. As you allowed your weight to dig into his lower back and his trapezius, you started hating yourself for doubting the gentle voice that told you something just wasn't right.

You went on his page again as soon as he left. Found nothing too suspicious. And yet you hired a private investigator—a sixty-year-old, retired Irish detective—remembering the voice called intuition hardly falls short.

In his email the detective was frank. Someone without sight could've seen through this guy, he wrote. The evidence was attached.

A wife—a dentist from Maryland with her own clinic in Prospect Heights. They lived in a Park Slope brownstone they had purchased just two years ago. They had separated in November, when she caught him sending emails to other women, but reconciled at the end of January. Since then, they had been at their happiest, that's what her Facebook statuses said when you looked her up. And yet you weren't the only otra.

There are two other women, the investigator added. Smart women—a PhD candidate at Cornell and a successful Curriculum Developer for Amazon. Smart women, the email stated, seeking emotionally intelligent men and finding sons of bitches. A shame.

It hurt. More than the longer relationships did. But you went to work. Even when you wanted to drown in quicksand for having let down your guard, for being masterfully played, you knew only you could save you and so you carried on.

Giving into the hurt sometimes worked.
This time it wouldn't.

The women in your generation are unafraid once they choose to end cycles by holding the lessons they learn.

Build your own sense of self. Do not seek lanes that are not yours.

Listen to the voice—the subtle one.

Bodysuit

The outfit La Jefa got us for Memorial Day
weekend is a royal blue, long sleeved bodysuit
with silver trimmings. I wear see through
stockings to hide the appearance of cellulite. La
Jefa claims that when she orders these outfits she
tells the seamstress to make the bottoms into shorts
and it's only because our asses are so grandiose
that they ride up and become thongs. We all know
she be lying. Pero it works, she claims, you want
the bigger tips, si o no?

☾

When Mami found out Lisbel was a girl she
said, Bueno, that I can do. I know how to raise
those without un hijo de la gran puta. She rubbed
my head softly and placed my hand on her belly.
Lisbel's foot pushed off my palm as she kicked
wildly. Chiquita, I said, I will always have your
back.

Now, Lisbel is in college and always asks me questions that make me feel dirty. It's not her intention, I know that, but I feel it in the tone she uses. I don't know if it was college or entre Mami and my tías, but she has been taught to judge me. Her Instagram profile has quotes from women like Bell Hooks and Cherrie Moraga— women I have never heard of before I search them up and realize I know nothing. Her profile icon is an image of women's fists in different shades of brown against a hot pink background. Once I told her that women like Cardi B are feminist too. And she said, obvio que someone who didn't finish college thinks that. When I cursed her out, she laughed and pretended she meant it as a joke. I let it go.

☾

Cardi B's "Bickenhead" is blasting when I walk into Cosmos, the club I work in. I approach the women, the ones who I have created bonds with because they do not make threats when their customers choose to be served by me once in a blue. In all honesty, nosotras sabemos que los hombres son asi—today it's you, tomorrow it's otra. We greet each other careful not to ruin our faces. It's the song we have chosen since the album came out to warm up to. The bartender props her leg on the sink and twerks and immediately we are hyping her up in unison. I dance my way to the locker room glancing at the other girls, the ones who hurl threats quicker than they take breaths when their regulars look anywhere that isn't them. They take selfies or make videos to post up. Ain't nobody got time for that.

The locker room is so bright it burns my eyes, but I know the lighting is perfect to apply foundation.

What's your goal this weekend, Uribel? Rubia asks. She's the only one here that has earned la confianza to call me by my first name. She sits on the chair next to mine and applies a red lip.

$3,000, girl, and that's a reach, I reply. I dab on some concealer under my eyes.

It can be six, she says. Rubia is Colombian and always has access to real bank. She can afford to actually give zero fucks about the competition and pettiness in this place; a privilege she never fails to remind me she worked hard to gain. On my first shift, she gave me the best piece of advice I've gotten to date when I almost got into a fight con una tipa that appeared friendly at the beginning of the night. In the locker rooms, she said, everyone es gran amiga, but out on the floor, it's vicious— especially for buenamosas like you.

I shake my head. I don't knock the hustle, Rubia, It's just not for me right now. I always add the right now part is an add on because I never know when I might change my mind; Mami is getting older, and I don't want Lisbel to struggle to work and go to college. On top of that, I've worked all of my life. God knows I want a little luxury, a little comfort, from now until the end of my days.

I have seen a lot of women come and go. Within the same minute, your self-esteem can be inflated and popped. It's why so many of us run back to the island and come back with the bodies we need to stand at the front lines. The gig isn't for everyone. The music is loud, and every time you go to a table to take orders the men rest their hand on the dip of your back, too close to the region of your ass or on your shoulders too close to your chest. It took me three months to get used to having my ass groped and my tits dique accidentally squeezed. Rubia taught me how to use those moments to slip my hands into pockets; touch never be free. The money helped my discomfort. By my sixth month, I was making enough to give a cut to a security to keep an eye on my tables. Now, I am touched only cuando me dan las ganas. Lisbel might say all she wants to say, but she isn't taking out loans because of me. $3,000 to serve bottles on the weekend, why the fuck not? I will not complain. I wish she would actually say something.

℃

Lisbel is up scrambling eggs when I get home a little after six in the morning. Although she has a perfectly good room at Mami's, she decides to crash on the couch on the weekends to catch up on her shows. Mami refuses to add any services to the cable. La cosa dique ta' mala, pero none of that stops her from taking frequent trips back home on my dollar. I take off my coat and my hoodie, peel off my sweats. Uribel, is that what you wore all night? she asks. Her eyebrow is arched and her lips are pressed.

Yep, this was the outfit, I take a breath. Bueno.

Bueno what, Lisbel?! I yell—tired, hungry, and annoyed. You are so passive aggressive lately. What is it with you?

No. Whatever, if you feel comfortable, do you, she slams the skillet into the sink.

HELLO, HELLO! I'm trying, pero tu no me dejas! You're always coming out your face or looking at me in some kind of way.

That's your own stuff. Figure that out, sis. She turns around and walks into the living room. I follow.

Na, that's you, I say. You gotta problem with how I make a living? I try to remember she is almost ten years younger than me. That in all honesty she's just a little girl, but my ears are burning with rage.

Would you regularly wear that? She pops a piece of egg into her mouth.

No, have you seen me wear something like this?

You wouldn't because you know it's vulgar.

Bitch, this vulgar outfit made me $2,500 dollars all in one night. And guess where the fuck the stack to pay off your balance is coming from?

Don't throw that in my face.

So, get the fuck out my face with your bullshit, Lisbel! Stop treating me like I'm a maldito grillo. I live this lifestyle because it pays bank I wouldn't touch with a Ph-motherfucking-D. I'm not doing this shit for free.

I'm just saying you'll be thirty soon. No one is going to be checking for you if you out here looking like, she points the remote at my body and swings it up and down.

Lena Dunham's voice comes off the TV. If I were who I was just a year ago, I'd smash the remote on her head. Pero, I take a deep breath, walk over to her, take the plate from her hands. Get out of my apartment, Lisbel. She tells me to stop exaggerating and to let her be. I pull her off the couch and push her towards the door, where she steps into her Uggs.

¡You come back when you can show some respect, chamaquita e' mierda, coño! I yell through the window when I see her exiting the building. I can't help but laugh as I bring down the window— Every day more I become my mom.
When I turn to the television Dunham is running through a suburban area with no bottoms and a hoodie on. Rolling my eyes, I turn the whole TV off. I've tried to watch this show with Lisbel before, but it irritates me that abortions and drug use in those women can be broadcasted without judgement.

I throw some hot sauce on Lisbel's remaining eggs and bring them to my mouth with my fingers as I phone Rubia. Anything for tonight? I ask her leaning over my kitchen counter. She says there is—some ball players are coming through the city and there's a private affair. Nada forzado, Morena, she adds. I tell her I'll be there—I got bills

to pay, people to take care of, and places to see.
This is my body, my choice.

    If feminism is not rooting for me to fill in
the gaps in whatever way I can, then feminism ain't
for me. Theories ain't no real answer for the
women I know. I might not have a fancy degree,
pero I know it is only through actual action we
survive.

The Ride on the Yamaha

You are 24 riding on the back of a Yamaha motorcycle with a dress on. The dress has colorful flowers falling on a dark background. Thinking about the femininity this nine-dollar dress would lend you, you picked it up. Underneath it, you've got shorts on. A year ago, you finally learned about the burn your legs cause each other if you don't give them their space. The shorts cut into your thick thighs like rubber bands except it doesn't hurt. It feels like freedom because you're crossing a bridge on a motorcycle, and the cold air is grasping you in between gushes of hotness. You're 24. You might never live moments like these again, so you inhale deep. The roaring and humming of the Yamaha echoes in your skull and it resonates with something inside of you- you don't have a clue just what, but you sense it. You look at the city of Manhattan as if the lights were stars. The

Pepsi-Cola sign is on fire or maybe just lit red. You don't care. He touches your bare thigh with his gloved hand as he comes to a red light. People in the car to your left look, discreetly point with their noses, and talk. Their heads are covered. Where would modesty take you? You're going to remember this moment forever even when it breaks. You don't know about the breaking yet.

The guy whose chest your arms are holding onto isn't the same one you expected. But in just a few hours, you'll see that sometimes good guys with budding commitment issues are not compatible with recovering broken girls. And yet, you'll cherish his presence in the memory of the Yamaha. You'll place him on a pedestal when you tell stories of him because in reality, he wasn't that bad. He took you places and dressed you in affection, and eventually it won't matter whether he meant what you thought he meant or not. He was just him, great for himself, great for memories-- not a place for you to build a foundation on. At first, you'll struggle with this truth. For a few days, you'll try to change it because he's charming, and you almost believe he will do. But he won't. Things like this you will begin to be ok with, even if you are not accepting of it on the back of the Yamaha.

Eventually you'll truly begin to appreciate people for who they are and the purpose they serve. You'll stop comparing their actual size to the size you thought they were. It will be all good. You'll remember Manhattan and how it looks when you leave it for Queens. You'll remember the car of

Muslim men and women who stopped with you at the red light and snickered because your legs were exposed and opened wide against the back of a man, and their heads were covered. Both of you failed to realize then that you roamed the same city looking for a place of rest. You'll remember the Yamaha and the guy. You'll remember the anxiety in your body to get to his place. To have him rip off your dress and plunge into you. You'll remember that he was always quick but, on this night, he held on long enough to ask you who you belonged to between moans in broken Spanish. And all you wanted to do was say that you belonged to you. Because you wanted him to come already, you lied. You'll remember all of this. And it will always make you smile because...

You'll remember the voice that told you to hold on to the moment on the Yamaha. You'll remember awareness. You'll remember the point in time when everything was too much but just right, and you finally had a small moment to wave at yourself.

Hi.

Sometimes we forget about ourselves when we are in the web of the beginning stages of relationships. You do that often. Straighten out your curls because he mentioned he likes it straight more. Attempt to look more natural in photographs because he's mentioned he can tell when you pose.

☾

Almost three years now, and the Yamaha is gone. He sold it before moving across the country. Long before that, you had stood him up on countless dates, so he wrote a text that read more like a yearbook sign off.

☾

I think you have a thing for moments and memories—even when they break. In fact, you'll figure out that there is an underlying reason why you might like them a little better then.

You

"No creo que yo esté aquí demás.
Aquí hace falta una mujer, y esa mujer soy yo."
-Aida Cartagena Portalatin

You learn that mornings feel good in your own bed, with clean sheets and the plants you tend to humming in your face. You figure out that making your own tea or being served coffee depends on your mood, and that is ok. You adapt and constantly move your body for the feelings to flow, for the solutions to grow. You begin to accept being split in two, in four, in six—just as long as you hold on to the one root that is you.

You dream of cousins revealing to you they are confused and hurt, and their vulnerability alarms a feeling that seems distant. You familiarize yourself with waking up and telling yourself you no longer carry anyone else's pain. You gain the ability to put yourself back to sleep touching the parts that feel good or by tuning into your own heartbeat. You learn to breathe through pleasure instead of holding your breath like you did through pain.

You understand that motivation is nothing without discipline so you do the things you must do every day without skipping. You forgive yourself quicker than you did when you end a streak. You become the person you want to be.

You are a solid individual. Solid. Strong. Now, no one, not even death, can shake you. You have looked at your past, moved through the toxic survival skills you had to push down your throat. You have taken the lessons and made them into gold bracelets that hang around your wrist, a reminder even when you rest, a reminder even when your heart is filled for a someone else outside of yourself.

You have taught yourself to curve your tongue and circle your lips to say no. You say no to all the things that do not consider you.

You walk to parks. You dance. You sit. You read. You write. You love. You love the woman who pushed you rigid into the world and the man that exploded you into the vessel. You acknowledge that their ignorance hurt and nurtured you. You forgive them for not having known and for not doing better by you when you needed them. You take accountability. You say sorry to those you hurt in your growing. You let your siblings know you care. You hold your sister when she is weak and when she is drenched in strength. You let her show you her own majesty. You learn to be ok putting your head on her shoulder.

You don't have to be alone anymore, so you walk to the living room, stretch your hand into his, and he holds it. You don't have to speak. You let the sunshine baptize the both of you, melt the blood that has gone solid overnight into free-flowing liquid once more. You know you no longer have to hide. You say something feels different this morning and lay your head on his lap as you try to figure it out.

You remember that last night someone named you, and you wanted to come out your skin. You swallowed your water instead of hurling your power at them. You tell him this and he strokes your hair. You say that next time you will speak. You silence is not always growth. That thing that keeps your lips sealed, it is something called fear. You regret not speaking, you regret biting your tongue, having tamed yourself in the name of a superficial peace. You look at him, and he tells you he is there to listen, but only you know how to re-calibrate out of this.

You walk to your bed. You open your journal. You breathe and you write, and you stretch like a cat.

You know what it is like to be touched
      and taken after you say no.
You know what it is like to scream
      and not be heard.
You know what it is like to press your legs together until
      they lock, and your hips hurt.
You know what it is like to stand with your mother in
      the winter on the welfare lines on Fordham
      Road.
You know what is like to hear her tell the vecina to let
      her pride down, to ask for help by standing in
      the cold, too.
You know the joy of the first of the month and the rush
      to the supermarkets that sell twenty plátanos for
      a dollar.
You know what it is like to miss the island even when
      your mother says she doesn't.
You know the reward of section eight housing after your
      father beat your mother blue.

You know what it is like to see your mother rejoice and
      say, "Aunque sea sirvió pa' algo."
You know visiting your father in jail and touching his
      orange clothes.
You know rushing, climbing, and scratching the guards
      with your little sister while yelling for them to
      let your daddy go.
You know what it is like to have the government deport
      him.
You know what it is like to hear a grown man tell you, a
      child, that one of his women has put a spell on
      him and so he'll die in the next few days.
You know what is like to have your mother hold your
      hands together as she announces he is gone.
You know what is like to be hungry and have jeans with
      holes on the inside of your thick thighs.
You know what it is like to have kids make fun of your
      fat, of your textured hair, of your big lips, of the
      way your eyebrows touch.
You know what it is like to hate your cousins for having
      dads.
You know what is like to be kicked out of a public school.
You know how to cut parts of you just to feel loved by
      your own blood.
You know watching your mother faint at the sight of
      death on you.
You know how to use your trauma for financial aid and
      stipends.
You know the sound of white kids scoffing at your
      answers during class discussions.
You know what it is like to have a professor tell you your
      personal essay does not leave space for
      resolutions.

You know being fired for calling a priest Mister instead
   of father.
You know how to shake your ass, give happy endings,
   and fake relationships for some dollars.
You know what it is like to have handcuffs on you and be
   thrown into a cage.
You know what it is like to fight other women on the
   four train over a man.
You know what is like to have that man beat, spit, and
   drag you.
You know what it is like to go back to him and beg for
   forgiveness.
You know that the most vulnerable version of your
   mother is the lowest version of you.
You know what it is like to leave before misery makes
   her kill.

You know.
You know.
You know.

You know what it is like to sit in the silence, to have
   your thoughts do backflips and cartwheels all
   while reminding you of all you aim to forget.
You know what it is like to wake up anyway.
You know how to verbalize what hurts.
You know how to find a therapist.
You know how to pray.
You know how to stretch your limbs and twist your back.
You know how to ask for what it is you want.
You know how to reach for help and how to give without
   hitting empty.

You know how to breathe through pleasure and fright.
You know how to walk away from what isn't in your
        highest good and how to walk into challenges
        that accelerate growth.
You know how to apologize.
You know how to listen without a response.
You know how to set boundaries so you can thrive
        instead of always having to survive.
You know how to begin to end generational traumas in
        you.
You know how to notice the trigger and their roots.
You know—

You pick up the phone. You dial the
number. You wait even though she sends you to
voicemail. You say what you need to say:

Hola Tía, espero que estes bien. Te quería decir
que it really bothered me last night that you said que yo
era malcriada porque no te besé la mano. La verdad es
que no te saludé porque estabas con una persona que me
causó mucho daño. I am just not at the place where I
can forgive him yet. In fact, sometimes I feel his
redemption is above me. Pero tu eres mi Tia, y me
quisiste cuando yo misma no me quería. No fué mi
intención que tu te sintieras not seen by me. Te veo
siempre—hasta cuando me miro en el espejo. I love you.
Tirame cuando puedas.

You hear the water running. You see the
tub filled with honey, rose water, and stardust.
You know that outside, at any moment, the war can
break wide open or peace can infiltrate, and your

home will always be a sanctuary. You know you
have built this place with your words and the
facing of the spaces in you. You feel his arms
draped around your hips, and you turn your head
to kiss him. You ask him to stay.

> You know.
> You know.
> You know.

You know managing and coping will only convert
open wounds to small aches. You know shifts end
but no part of you is ever complete.

> You know that Malcriadas
> can love the world
> awake.

●

Reader—if you are anything like the characters, if you grew up in similar circumstances, I hope these stories may have entered your wounds as an elixir sent to affirm and heal—like the stories I hold nearest to my own heart. If you are not like the characters on these pages, if you did not grow up with experiences that mirror these or if they just did not resonate in the slightest bit, may they have driven you to discomfort and empathy.

Take what you need and leave the rest.

With gratitude y fortaleza,

LA
Lory
Lorena
Lorraine
Ms. Avila
Lorraine Avila

Acknowledgements

My **familia**: To **my Madre, Taty,** and **my padre, Felix**. My parents who did the best they could even when it wasn't enough. My parents who never doubted I could do anything I wanted whether it be teaching, going back to school, moving across the country, or starting over again. Every ounce of courage I have in me has been gathered through the fact that their love is a net I have that holds me and propels me forward.
To **my Papi, Miguel Avila**, may you RIP. I carry so much of you in me. Our trips to the library weren't in vain. Thank you for forcing me to read and write at an early age. Thank you for having my back from wherever it may be that you are. To **Tatiana**, my sister. I don't love anyone else in the world the way I love you. You have been the only one who has shared all of my homes, and thus knows all of me. To my **nephews and nieces,** you have challenged me to be the best role model I can be. Malcriadx or not, I love you, I got you, I see the best in you. We, the adults in your life, are genuinely trying the best we can even though it may not always be enough. To my cousins, **Diana, Daribel, Shamel, and Ashley**—you are the blood in my veins. It turns out I don't really need friends I already have all of you—ha! Thank you for growing alongside me and seeing me as my whole self. Thank you for listening to my ideas and reading and editing my stories. Thank you for teaching me how to love, fight, and love again :) To

Madrina Sisa, thank you for always having encouraged me to love the melanin in my skin, to be fearless and independent. Thank you for doing everything to turn La Capital upside down that time I was kidnapped (that story is for another book). To my **Tia Belkis**, thank you for listening to my nightmares. Thank you for holding me when I've been too weak to admit I was hurting and for opening your doors to me always. To **Tia Minut**, bless you for buying me my first (Garfield themed) journal! To **Padrino**—gracias por siempre buscar maneras de ponerme comoda. To **Shadhey**, thank you for your lessons. You are my forever angel.

To **Dominican Writers**—thank you for believing in my voice as a writer and taking a chance on me. **Angy Abreu**, I appreciate your patience, vulnerability, and expertise. You have pushed me out of my comfort zone and I'll never return again! **Sydney Valerio**, thank you for easing me into revising knowing that even work that just seems tedious can take an emotional toll.

To **Crystal Rodriguez** thank you for your art, for saying yes, for creating visuals that seek to have the audience understand my stories through a visual lens.

To **Jennifer Colon**. For being a full friend. For listening. For helping me manifest the book tour as we traveled through Central America—where is my banda now, eh? May we continue discovering the worlds within ourselves.

To **Nia Thomas**. I manifested a friend to share my stories with. You are it—it was worth the wait. Thank you, querida! Next to all those who hyped up and encouraged the development of my voice throughout the years, especially (in no particular order):

To **Johanna Estevez** for accompanying me into the wounds that worked to keep my healing stagnant. For letting me guide myself into my own cure. My healing has been expedited, and I know better than to say I owe it to you :)

To **The Wing** for this WHOLE ASS scholarship. I am writing from the San Francisco branch at this very moment. In fact, I have weaved this entire manuscript from this space. The Wing gave me the seat, comfortability, wine, coffee, and energy I needed to get this done...pero we gon' need more seats :)

To **the Bronx** for being the reason I GO SO HARD! Thank you for the scars, for the blocks, for raising me up even when our foundation was handed to us shaken. **The Island, Quisqueya,** for your magic, for your wisdom, for your perseverance. To the **Bay Area**—my first home away from New York. Thank you, a million times, for comforting me with your distinct diaspora, for welcoming me in, for giving me the space I needed from home to begin to heal and tie together these narratives. For all those who have encouraged my writing:

First of all, to **my former middle school students** who thought everything I wrote as a model was genius and always asked for more! **Jehan Giles, Sabrina Paulino, Shyla Espejo, Melanie Martinez, Anybel Alfonso, Kulwa Apara, Chabely Rodriguez, Gabby Rivera, Elizabeth Acevedo, Belinda Bellinger, Zahira Kelly, Kamaria Carnes, Erica Buddington, Alida Reyes, Amanda Rosado, Amanda Alcántara, Danyeli Rodriguez Del Orbe, Vanessa Martir, Alicia Anabel Santos. My high school teachers at Bronx Academy of Letters: Desiree Battaglia, Ameer Kim El-Mallawany, Mitra Lucas, and Sarah Leistikow. My college professors: Dr. Anthony Lioi and Meera Nair. My Oakland roommate gang! And everyone who has ever said a kind thing about the writing I have shared on social media :)**

For all of those authors who have *deeply* inspired my writing: **Roxanne Gay, Ana Castillo, Toni Morison, Angie Cruz, Josefina Baez, Sandra Cisneros, Akwaeke Emezi, Anjali Sachdeva, Julia Alvarez, Nelly Rosario, Chimamanda Ngozi Adichie, Elizabeth Acevedo, Junot Diaz, Yaa Gyasi, Isabel Allende, Audre Lorde, Zora Neale Hurston, Jesmyn Ward, Tayari Jones.**

To **me and the Gods in me** cause díme.

Lorraine   Avila   is a writer, the daughter of Dominican immigrants, and an educator. She was born and raised in the Bronx, New York. The diasporic moves of those that came before her have deeply influenced her writing.

Lorraine graduated from Fordham University with a degree in English and Middle East studies and a minor in Creative Writing. She received her Master's degree from New York University in Secondary Education.   In 2019, she became a recipient of the The Wing's Scholarship Program. Her writing has been featured in *Hippocampus Magazine, Moko Magazine, The GirlMob, La Galería Magazine,* and *Blavity.*

www.LorraineAvila.com
Instagram/Twitter: Lorraineavila_
lorraineaviladlc@gmail.com

CPSIA information can be obtained
at www.ICGtesting.com
Printed in the USA
FSHW021904160919
62054FS